"What egotism," Meli mocked lightly.

"I can see the pulse in your throat and I know what it would feel like under my lips, beating so wildly with the passion I can arouse in you." His eyes promised her that passion, and the stars and moon, too.

"I've never denied that you can excite me," she stated with absolute calm, cursing the pulse that gave her away.

"Let it happen," he cajoled in utterly seductive cadences. "One last perfect night to remember."

She felt herself swaying against him. It would be so easy, so very easy to give in to what he wanted . . . what she wanted, too. . . .

LAURIE PAIGE

was born on a farm in Kentucky, the youngest of seven children. She and her husband worked their way through college, and she draws on these experiences as well as those of working as a reliability and data systems engineer on the Space Shuttle for her stories.

Dear Reader,

Silhouette Special Editions are an exciting new line of contemporary romances from Silhouette Books. Special Editions are written specifically for our readers who want a story with heightened romantic tension.

Special Editions have all the elements you've enjoyed in Silhouette Romances and *more*. These stories concentrate on romance in a longer, more realistic and sophisticated way, and they feature greater sensual detail.

I hope you enjoy this book and all the wonderful romances from Silhouette.

Karen Solem
Editor-in-Chief
Silhouette Books

LAURIE PAIGE
Lover's Choice

Silhouette Special Edition
Published by Silhouette Books New York
America's Publisher of Contemporary Romance

Silhouette Books by Laurie Paige

Gypsy Enchantment (DES #123)
South of the Sun (ROM #296)
Lover's Choice (SE #170)

SILHOUETTE BOOKS, a Division of Simon & Schuster, Inc.
1230 Avenue of the Americas, New York, N.Y. 10020

ISBN: 0-671-53670-2

First Silhouette Books printing June, 1984

10 9 8 7 6 5 4 3 2 1

Map by Ray Lundgren

America's Publisher of Contemporary Romance

Printed in the U.S.A.

Lover's Choice

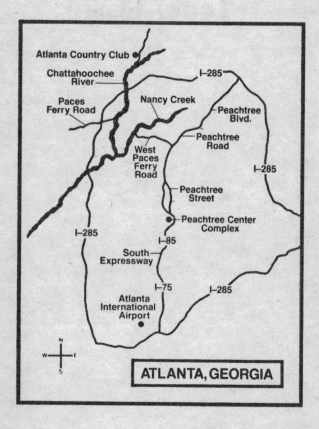

Atlanta Country Club •
Chattahoochee River
Paces Ferry Road
Nancy Creek
I-285
Peachtree Blvd.
Peachtree Road
West Paces Ferry Road
Peachtree Street
I-285
Peachtree Center Complex
I-285
I-85
South Expressway
I-75
I-285
Atlanta International Airport •
N
W E
S

ATLANTA, GEORGIA

Chapter One

*M*eli O'Connor replaced the hairbrush on the shelf above the commode and leaned close to the mirror mounted over the bathroom sink to study her hair color. She decided she liked the new shampoo-in coloring she had used this time.

Normally, her hair was what she classified as "dirty blond." The shampoo had turned the sun-bleached top layers to light gold and the hidden bottom ones to burnished gold. Bangs feathered across her forehead from a side part, helping disguise the heart-shaped lines which she thought weren't strong enough for the owner of a vacation retreat–fishing camp.

She reached over to the shelf and picked up a round brush that lay next to the regular one she had been using. With sure, skillful movements, she curled the ends of her medium-length hair under with the brush and used the hot air from her blow-dryer to set the style. In a couple of minutes she had completed the task.

She removed the towel wrapped sarong-fashion around her and hung it to dry on the bar of the shower door. She went into her bedroom, stepped into a flannel granny gown, slipped it up over her shoulders, and buttoned the front opening up to her neck. She pulled on quilted, ankle-high booties and silently went out and down the narrow wooden steps into the living room.

The clock on the mantel showed a minute after ten, and a new program had just started on TV.

Since she wasn't at all sleepy, she opened the fire screen, tossed another log on the fire, poked it into flame, then settled on the comfortable sofa with her legs stretched out. Her smoky blue eyes reflected the glow of the embers as she stared into the fireplace rather than at the TV screen.

Beyond the double-insulated storm windows, darkness etched the forest with deep shadows. A new snow from the night before cloaked the valley and the rise of mountains that surrounded it. The silence was a tangible thing, touching the rustic, two-level cabin on all sides.

Absently, she rose, turned off the television and the only lamp that had been on, and resumed her seat.

The atmosphere of tranquility was deceiving. Deep inside Meli was a confusing mixture of emotions—disappointment because the weather would keep Tor from showing up and relief because she wasn't sure she wanted to see him. Her decision was too new. She needed time to reinforce it.

Not that she hadn't given sufficient thought to the project; she had been thinking about it for a year now. With the coming of springtime, she had made a definite commitment: she was going to get married again.

All she needed to do was to find a husband. That was where Tor would be useful. A rueful smile caused her lips to move a tiny bit.

Lights flashed against the night, catching her attention. Meli got up and watched from a front window as a vehicle made its way slowly along the one-lane road leading into the camp. The muffled groan of an engine fighting its way through five inches of powdery snow was interspersed with the *whomp-whomp* sound of chain-clad tires.

Surprise, then disbelief, widened Meli's eyes as the four-wheel-drive Jeep turned into her driveway and stopped and a tall, bulky figure emerged, stretching his arms over his head in a gesture of weariness.

"Tor!" she cried, yanking open the front door and pushing outward on the storm door. Flipping on the porch light, she waited, the freezing cold air swirling under her nightgown to wring a shiver from her slender form.

The man leaned into his auto, grabbed a small suitcase, and ran clumsily through the crusted snow, cursing and laughing under his breath as he did.

He leaped up the three steps in one bound and

stomped the clinging, sugary snow from his boots. Then he curved one long arm around Meli's waist, lifted her from the floor, and carried her inside, letting the storm door close of its own accord while he gave the inner door a backward kick.

"Tor Halliday! What are you doing here in this weather?" she demanded, laughing as he swung her around and around, his face buried in the curve of her neck, his nose chilling the warm skin there as he nuzzled her.

He tossed the suitcase onto a lowboy beside the entrance and used both arms to gather her warm body into his embrace. His lips sought along her jaw until he found the treasure.

Meli gave herself to the kiss, opening her lips beneath his cold ones and answering the stroking caress of his tongue with her own. She shivered as the chill from his nylon parka penetrated her nightgown.

"Sorry, babe," he murmured, releasing her.

He unzipped the coat after removing his gloves and tossing them next to his suitcase. The coat soon joined the gloves.

Meli untied his hiking boots and helped him to get out of them, then placed the boots on a shelf under the lowboy seat to dry.

She had just returned to an upright position when she was scooped into Tor's strong arms. He carried her across the room and sank onto the sofa, holding her hugged to his powerful chest with a demanding ardor. His cobalt blue eyes burned over her with a hunger that never failed to kindle her passion to a white-hot pitch to match his.

Briefly, she wondered about the etiquette of asking a lover to help her find a husband. Perhaps she should find an appropriate book that advised one on the protocol for such delicate matters.

Manners were momentarily forgotten when his arms tightened around her slender rib cage as if he knew of her inattention. She locked her arms around his shoulders and lifted her face for his kiss. Little impulses of desire flittered throughout her at the mastery in his touch. He knew her so well.

"Do you realize it's been over a month?" he asked, a note of grievance in his voice, as if it had somehow been her fault that he hadn't been able to break away from his many business enterprises to come here.

"I didn't expect you, with this snow and all," she gasped as he gave her an undignified squeeze that forced what little breath she had left out of her lungs.

"I've been driving for hours through the damned stuff. I nearly didn't make it." His stroking, sensitive fingers began an exploration along her sides. "I wish the camp was closer to the airport," he said in resigned exasperation.

"You shouldn't have taken up with a woman who lives in the north woods of Montana. One in Atlanta would have been more practical," she advised airily.

Once she had thought there was another woman in Georgia, but, for no particular reason except that

Tor seemed to be with her every spare minute he had, she no longer thought that. If the person named Mary Beth had been part of his life at one time, she was definitely part of his past now—which could make Meli's own decision harder for him to take.

"Yeah," he agreed in soft, drawling tones which were deeper, quieter when he was making love to her. "But you've ruined me for anyone else." This he admitted with a rueful chuckle.

Meli loved his voice. It seemed to have a wealth of undertones: sometimes murmuring darkly like the secretive chuckling of the mountain brooks that ran over the round, greenish stones of the streambeds; sometimes sounding wistful like the sigh of the wind through the evergreens. At other times, especially when he laughed, his voice was like the clear notes of a brass wind chime, deep and mellow.

"Enchanted is the correct term, I believe," he continued, his eyes narrowing as they swept down her unsexy night attire in an intense perusal that confused and excited her at the same time.

Catching his face between her hands, she raised herself to kiss him and then asked, "Do you need anything? Some hot tea?"

"Only you," he murmured, trapping her bottom lip between his strong teeth before she could withdraw. "But some tea would be nice."

He heaved himself up with her still in his arms and carried her into the kitchen. Refusing to release her, he walked to the stove, let her turn the heat on under the kettle, then, still holding her, let her prepare their cups. It wasn't until she threatened mutiny that he permitted her to slide from his arms to the floor.

When she placed the cups of steaming tea on the table, he again pulled her into his lap to hold her while they drank.

"Sure you don't want something to eat now?" she asked, half teasing.

His eyes answered her. One large hand rubbed up and down her back in a gentling motion, as if he were taming her to his touch. He was always gentle with her when they came together.

"How did the labor negotiations turn out?" she asked. How was she going to lead up to her decision and the request for his help? "I kept track of the news on TV, but the reporters didn't know much, except that you had reached an agreement."

"I was satisfied with the final draft of the contract, but we're coming close to pricing ourselves right out of the world market. Never mind," he growled, swooping down on her vulnerable neck, his lips tracing moist kisses along the smooth skin. "I'm not interested in the world or the labor force or anything else—only in a tiny scrap of woman who draws me again and again to the wilds of Montana." His kisses increased in fervent demand. With sudden movements, Tor rose from the kitchen chair, taking her with him in his powerful arms. "I need you," he said thickly, all play and patience gone. "I need you, babe."

Carrying her, he made his way lightly across the living room and up the six narrow steps to her bedroom, where he dropped her in the middle of the bed. He stood on the thick, furry rug for a long minute, drinking his fill of the peace of the room as he looked around for changes that might have occurred in his absence.

Meli understood that he was absorbing something he needed. Lying quietly, she studied him, noting the expressions crossing his face, the deepening of desire in his eyes. She knew him well, yet found him to be a contradiction in so many ways.

He had often shown himself perceptive where she was concerned. Maybe he would understand her need to have someone of her own. But he could be possessive, she acknowledged.

Six feet five inches tall, with light blond hair and dark blue eyes, he looked like a Norseman. In fact, his grandmother had come from Denmark, hence his name. But he had been raised in the South. His home was in Atlanta and that was where he ran his giant corporation, Southern Companies Limited. She had never understood the "Limited" part, since he dealt in everything from manufacturing to mining.

In his black and red plaid shirt, which he was now throwing at a chair, and his tight jeans, he looked like a lumberjack, but this impression was contradicted by his somewhat lean face, a face with an aesthetic quality that was indescribably but compellingly masculine.

He shucked his pants, leaving them on the carpet. His T-shirt, shorts, and socks landed in a heap on top of the jeans. Then he paused, standing there as proud as his namesake, Thor, the Norse god of thunder.

He was a true blond, his body hair only a few shades darker than that on his head and lighter than her own. Little flames danced in her blood as he looked down at her reclining form, watching her as she waited for him.

"You're as beautiful as I remember, witch of the north woods," he murmured.

"And you," she whispered, returning the compliment as her eyes ran over his tall, lean form. His body was strong and hard, with long, supple lines, like that of a runner.

He raised one knee to the bed and rested his weight on it as his hand reached down to sweep along the length of thigh visible in outline against the soft material of her nightgown. Deftly he pulled off the quilted booties that she wore and flipped them to the floor beside his apparel.

"I have a present for you," he said softly.

Her eyes flicked in amusement to his face. "I can see that," she said, with laughter ruffling her voice.

His grin was wry. "Besides that."

The passion that filled his hard male body was impossible for him to hide. His hands began a thorough search of her through the gown as he knelt beside her on the bed.

"I need to make sure everything is still the same." He chuckled suddenly, unexpectedly. "My dreams have been tormenting me this past month. For some reason I kept dreaming that when I got here, you'd be gone." He worked on her buttons.

"But here I am," she reminded him, a tender smile lighting her gentle-featured countenance.

His gaze was momentarily fierce, like that of a golden eagle. "Yes." He spoke in a deep growl. Immediately softening, he smiled at her questioning look. "Don't mind me. I'm tired."

Her hands stroked his powerful thighs. "Perhaps you'd better get in bed and sleep."

Tor pushed her gown up. She raised her hips and then sat up so he could dispose of it. It, too, went on the floor.

"Not a chance," he whispered, his eyes full of longing. His hand on her shoulder guided her back against the fur throw. "Let me look at you, babe."

After a studious perusal that left her skin heated and yearning for his touch, he stretched out beside her, raising himself on one elbow. His free hand began a journey all its own, traveling from her shoulder along her collarbone to her throat, tracing a line from there down between her breasts.

Sliding over the satiny skin, he palmed one burgeoning mound, then the other, his hand covering each one easily for she was small, although exquisitely formed, with pale pink nipples.

Then, in a broad sweeping motion, with fingers fully extended, he caressed her ribs and abdomen, pausing only a moment longer at the sandy thatch, then continuing downward to explore the smooth thighs and shapely calves and ankles before returning upward in a meandering trail that left tiny thunderbolts playing along all her skin surfaces.

Meli enjoyed his tactile appraisal to the utmost,

thrilling to his obvious pleasure in her silky skin and feminine form.

"Oh, Tor," she sighed, a tremor invading her voice and her body as she writhed beside him. "Please."

She reached for him, sliding her hands around his waist and giving an imperative tug, wanting his powerful masculine length touching all of her.

His lips opened in a teasing smile belied by the smoldering, raw passion in the depths of his eyes. But he was a man used to being in control, and he wouldn't allow her to take charge and rush them.

"Patience, my love," he cautioned in chiding amusement, his breath lightly stroking her chest as he bent his head. "I'll make sure it's all there for you, little greedy one."

His face slowly descended until just the tip of his tongue flicked out and touched the tip of her breast.

She gasped excitedly. "But not until I'm out of my mind," she complained.

"So we'll both go a little insane together," he promised as his mouth closed over the delicate nipple.

It was beyond imagining, this passion that erupted between them each and every time they came together so that every encounter seemed new, a thing reborn. It wasn't as if they were new lovers, just met. Their affair had lasted two years, since Meli was twenty-seven.

His lips on one breast, his fingers on the other, were sending spirals of heat into her innermost parts, warming the central core of her womanhood, getting her ready for him. He excited her beyond reason.

Forming a little circle, his fingers closed on her nipple, giving it a tiny pull while his teeth nibbled on the other. It wouldn't take long for her to go completely crazy if he didn't stop soon.

Her fingers caught in the blond strands of his hair, demanding that he come to her. With a low groan, he rolled his body against hers while his mouth answered her summons to come to her lips. Even so, his lips didn't take hers completely, but still insisted on teasing in a loving fashion. He barely brushed the soft mouth that opened expectantly for his invasion. Instead, his caress touched all over her face before slowly, so very slowly, he returned to her mouth.

Like an eagle diving, expertly taking its prey, he dropped to her mouth with a surety of motion that told her he knew exactly what he was doing. In another second she was drowning in his desire, her arms going around his shoulders to clasp him more tightly to her straining form.

With effort, he pulled his lips from hers. "Easy, babe. Let's make it last," he ground out. "I've waited too long . . ." He panted lightly beside her ear, and her own breathing rate increased.

"How long are you staying?" she managed to ask.

"I don't know . . . the weekend, maybe longer. I'm expecting a call." He feathered kisses along the sensitive spot beneath her ear, pushing her golden-hued hair aside.

With light, caressing strokes, she pressed her fingers down his sides, over his rock-hard hips, onto his thighs. "Then we have time for everything," she reminded him. Moving slightly, she twisted her body to give her room, her fingers brushing his abdomen as she touched him intimately, eliciting a sighing gasp from him.

"Witch," he gritted in a deep throaty growl, biting on her lower lip.

His hand retaliated for her boldness by pinching a tender spot along her inner thigh. With a single nudge, he parted her legs, moving one lightly haired, muscular thigh between her smooth ones.

A surge of desire shook her lithe frame and she encouraged the mating of their bodies.

Tor caught her hands and held them in easy captivity over her head. Her smoky eyes opened and stared into his passion-dark ones. "No," he said firmly.

Meli smiled and forced herself to relax against him, knowing his tastes as well as her own. "All right, love."

His gaze roamed down her flushed skin. "I could make love to you forever. I don't want it to be over with a 'wham-bam' routine, even if we do have time after this to go slowly." He frowned. "I want to discover you again," he said slowly.

She was surprised. His strange and prophetic dream really did seem to be bothering him. She pressed her lips together against the chill that again swept over her scalp and spine. A sense of destiny rushing at them overcame her. His troubled spirit encompassed hers.

"Hold me," she pleaded. "Tor, hold me."

Slipping his arms under her, he eased his weight more onto her clinging form and, sensitive to her mood, let her lose herself in him.

After a long moment he began to press searching kisses along her neck again, guiding her past the momentarily troubled time into passion's domain once more.

As their mouths met in increasingly demanding kisses, Tor's careful fingers explored her until he was certain that she was ready for him.

Arching his body over hers, he moved into the embrace of her thighs and, with exquisite gentleness, entered her. Then he proceeded to drive her wild until he, too, lost his iron control. They took each other beyond reason into ecstasy.

A long time later he slid off the fake fur throw, picked her up, and carried her into the bathroom. He set her on her feet while he turned on the shower and adjusted the water flow. Then he lifted her again and took her into the small enclosure with him.

After giving her a quick wash, he bathed himself, then turned off the shower. After he had dried them and they had returned to the bedroom, he commanded her to wait and dashed down the steps into the living room, wearing only a towel around his lean hips.

He returned with his suitcase, opened it, and handed her a present wrapped in children's birthday paper. With an eager little laugh, Meli tore off the silly wrapping and held up a new pair of pajamas. They had feet in them.

"Couldn't you find anything brighter?" she asked

innocently, eyeing the bright blue flannel with yellow polka dots on it.

"I looked all over Macy's. That's the brightest they had."

He took them from her and held the bottoms while she slid her feet inside. Standing, she let him pull them over her hips and fasten the snap at her waist. The elastic band in the back section made them fit snugly to her figure. He put the top on her and buttoned it.

She wondered if he would be this skillful at dressing a child. Certainly he was an expert with women. With a catch in her voice, she asked, "You've been in New York?"

"For most of March, then back to Atlanta this past week." He rummaged in his case and found the pajamas that he wore around the house but not to bed. Pulling them on, he looked up to flash her a devastating grin. "Don't you people know it's spring? April is for showers, not blizzards," he complained.

Pushing her ahead of him, he trailed after her down the steps and out to the roomy kitchen. When he visited, they made love first and then fixed a meal. He never took the time to eat on the way.

"This is probably the last snow of the season," she said, apologizing for the inconvenience. It had been a mild winter.

Although she had thought this thing through and had adopted a calm, philosophical attitude, the reminder of the last snow brought a deep nostalgic sadness with it.

This was their last snow together, she reflected. The last time they would be together as lovers, maybe as friends; that would depend on Tor's attitude toward her announcement—when she got up enough courage to make it.

"I hope so," he said fervently, cutting through her introspection and bringing her back to the topic at hand. "I plan on coming up often this summer."

She felt a sinking sensation in the vicinity of her heart. "How long did it take you to get here from the airport?" she inquired, ignoring his other statement.

"Almost five hours. It would help if you would plow your road!" He made a severe face at her.

"Don't need to." She got out some leftover roast and put it and a butcher knife on the wooden table for him to slice while she sliced and toasted home-made bread. "The only people here now came before the snow. Some naturalists who tramp through the woods each day. The kids can use the truck to get to school. It has snow tires."

"How are the kids doing?" Deftly, he cut off several slices of beef for their sandwiches.

Meli seized on the subject, anything not to talk about what was foremost in her mind!

"Fine," she said. She padded to the refrigerator on her rubberized soles and got out his favorite brown mustard and the Polski Wyrob kosher dills that he liked with roast beef.

"Are they helping out?"

"Yes, too much. I had to call a meeting with all the Robinsons: Mom, Pop, and the three teenagers. I explained that they were doing far too much work and I couldn't possibly pay them for all the hours they put in."

Tor chuckled at this, his laughter deep and quiet, a rich sound in the homey comfort of the kitchen.

"Thank you for getting them for me," she said.

"It was your idea to hire a manager for the cabins and the store," he reminded her.

"Yes, but it was your idea to add the cabins to make the camp appealing for families as well as ardent fishermen. I needed the extra help for the enlarged store as well as the bait and tackle shop."

She made two sandwiches for him and one for herself, spreading the bread with a thick covering of mustard and then adding the pickles and chips on the side of the plates.

"Beer, Coke, or milk?" She paused at the fridge.

He considered. "Umm, milk at this hour," he decided. "How is Fletch doing?" He put the plates on the table and sat down in his usual place.

Meli, pouring two tall glasses of milk, screwed up her mouth in a thoughtful moue before smiling over her shoulder. "He's super," she said as she joined Tor in the feast.

Fletcher Robinson was the manager she had hired at Tor's suggestion a year ago. She had been leery at first, but the whole family was so grateful to her that it was embarrassing. Fletch was a reformed alcoholic.

"I was worried about him getting through the long nights of winter, but he came through like a trouper.

Not one slip! He and Greta are like newlyweds; they do everything together. He helps her clean the cabins; she scoops bait without one squeamish shudder when he needs her to." Her graceful laughter wafted through the warm-toned room, drawing a smile from her companion.

Tor nodded complacently. "I knew he was a good man. He just needed to get away from the pressures of the city and business life. Something more basic and relaxed was what he needed." He grimaced. "Don't we all!"

Meli knew that Tor had just described what he received from their relationship. She provided a moment out of time for him, a relaxing interlude for her work-harassed lover.

Swallowing past the tightness in her throat, she said, "I really like the teenagers. Sam, Troy, and Gretchen are lots of fun." She wiped her mouth, rolled her eyes expressively. "They tease me about my Santa Claus boyfriend!"

A heavy scowl settled on his clean-sculpted features. "What the hell does that mean?"

She giggled to show they meant no harm and that she didn't mind their quips. "That you drop in out of the blue, usually at night, leave me a present, and then take off again with hardly anyone realizing you've been here." She raised a dainty line of curving eyebrow. "I assure you—I know you've visited!"

Was now the time to bring up her decision? Glancing upward from the cover of her long, light brown lashes, she studied his face. He looked tired, and he was irritated about the Robinson children's remarks.

She experienced an answering irritation . . . with him.

Again she was aware of the contradictions that he presented as he sat across the table from her, his anger fading to a thoughtful expression in less than a minute. No matter how long or how well she knew him, there would always be surprises, moments when his reactions changed in unpredictable ways.

His way of speaking, the soft slurring of syllables, indicated a lazy, laid-back manner that was totally at odds with his real self; he was actually quick and decisive.

Her brief ruffle of emotion passed as she remembered a newspaper article written about him when he had acquired a new company. He was known in the industrial world as "a mover and a shaker." At thirty-four, he controlled one of the largest conglomerates that operated from his home state.

Some people thought he was ruthless, but Meli didn't. She knew he could be kind and considerate . . . as a lover and as a friend. In fact, he was her very best friend. But he would not tolerate deceit or a wishy-washy manner from his personal or business acquaintances, she was sure.

He hadn't started from scratch. The wealth he had inherited from his father's manufacturing company had been considerable. Then he had come into a large sum when his mother had died, leaving to him the money she had gotten after her divorce from her second husband. He had used the cash in several daring adventures that had paid off. Not caring if he lost it, he wasn't afraid to take risks and so had increased his own fortune many times over.

Most of his time was spent in his Atlanta and New York offices, with the side trips to Montana whenever he could work them in . . . and the weather permitted.

A smile curved the delicately shaped lips as she recalled that he usually managed to get through to the camp even if he had to use a snowmobile. He had done that once this past winter, surprising her when he showed up at the beginning of a blizzard that snowed them in for a week.

"What are you grinning about?" he said, demanding to be let into her private joke.

"You," she replied pertly. "You're like the postman. You always get through no matter what the weather is doing."

Tor's eyebrows and lashes were darker than hers, which had always fascinated her since he was lighter everywhere else. Now he raised one medium dark brow roguishly at her. "Does he get to spend the night?"

Meli shook her head, her face merry with laughter. "Have you ever found anyone here, Santa Claus?" she teased.

Immediately the merriment disappeared from him. "No," he admitted. He looked as though he would like to ask a more specific question.

That wasn't like him, Meli thought. If he wanted to know something, he didn't hesitate to ask, even about the most personal subject.

Thinking of their relationship brought her face to face with her announcement. Tor wouldn't appreciate her dithering about telling him her news. Making up her mind, she nodded affirmatively. She would definitely tell him . . . just before he left!

Yes, that was a good idea. Then he would have time away from her to mull it over, realize she meant it and that it was for the best, and maybe help her in the project. After all, finding a husband was a major undertaking, and she needed all the help she could get to find just the type she wanted. That was where Tor would come in. He was bound to know someone in his vast ring of business connections who would be right for Meli. She knew what qualities she wanted. . . .

"Are you ready to go to bed?" he asked. His gaze on her as he stood and carried the dishes to the sink was lambent, almost strange in its gentle regard. He let her precede him while he turned out the lights and checked the fire, making sure the protective screen was closed before he hurried up the short flight of stairs to the bedroom with the large bed that had been his first gift to her.

After bumping his head several times the first weekend he had spent with her, he had sent out an extra large bed to fit his tall frame before his next visit.

Meli was snuggled under the covers when he entered the room. Hastily he threw off his pajamas and slid into the welcoming warmth.

His tall body was uniformly tanned the color of stained oak, as if he swam without a suit back in his sunny Southland home. She had wondered about it but had never asked him. She rarely asked him anything personal about his life away from her. They often discussed business, though, and she knew in detail what he was planning long before his corporate officers knew.

He, of course, was fully cognizant of her business affairs. The first summer they had met had been shortly after her father had died and she had moved back here to claim her inheritance, deciding to stay and run the business herself. Tor had advised her extensively while she took over, helping her with the many forms required of a business that leased its land from the government in the Flathead National Forest next to Glacier National Park.

She had only once intruded into his life away from her.

Needing his advice, she had called his home in Atlanta. The man who answered the phone—she assumed he was the butler—told her that Tor was in his room and he would ring through. A woman had answered the phone.

Sounding very much at home in Tor's room, the woman, Mary Beth, said that Tor was in the shower, and could she take a message. Meli had reluctantly left her name, but he didn't return the call.

Meli had made no allusion to the call when next she saw him, and she never made the mistake of calling him again. Although she didn't think Mary Beth figured in his life now, Meli carefully kept to her own place, concluding that if Tor wanted her in other areas of his existence he would invite her there. The fact that he hadn't, proved her earlier insight to be correct: she provided a moment out of time for her busy tycoon.

"Ready for the light to go out?" he asked, reaching a long arm across her to the bedside lamp.

"Yes," she said as he snapped off the switch.

He pulled her against him in the darkness, his hands easily working their way under the pajamas he had brought her.

"You smell good," he murmured. "And your hair is pretty." He noticed things like that. His hands became more intimate and again she was caught off guard as he began the ritual of love play.

Usually he waited until morning before he made love to her again, his favorite time being right after breakfast. Then he would help her with the dishes and the straightening of the house before they planned an activity for their leisure time, or else he helped her with her work.

But now his desire wouldn't wait as he tossed back the bedcovers and pulled the pajama bottoms off in one smooth, impatient motion. She was completely receptive to his touch.

"God, I've missed you," he muttered, his lips seeking hers in a kiss that left them both breathless. "I thought I'd never get to you . . ."

His voice trailed off as he paved a path of hot, moist kisses along her throat; his nimble fingers unfastened her buttons so he could continue to her breasts, which were budded with anticipation of his caresses.

A touch of sadness added to the piquancy of her

desire, making her response more fiercely demanding than it had ever been with him.

"Witch," he murmured, pulling the covers over them much later. "Wanton witch of the north," he said, chuckling with male contentment.

And at last they slept, the silence around them absolute in the hours before dawn.

Chapter Two

*M*eli, dressed in jeans, a blue knit turtleneck under a red and blue shirt with rolled-back cuffs, and nylon trail shoes, was in the kitchen reading the morning paper. It was after eleven, but Tor wasn't up yet. She let him sleep, knowing he needed the rest.

Suddenly his hands reached around her, crossing in front of her chest to grasp her arms as his lips nibbled along her cheek. She jumped slightly in surprise. "Tor!" she exclaimed, pleased that he was up and about.

"What's for breakfast?" He bit more daringly along her neck. "Umm, you taste good."

She squirmed out of his embrace, pushing him into his chair. "I have pancakes ready. And sausage."

She hurried to the oven and removed the two plates with their meal attractively arranged on them, plunked them down on the table, and poured big glasses of milk as well as mugs of coffee before she returned to her place.

Today he was wearing jeans, jogging shoes, and a shirt of tawny gold over a T-shirt, and he looked extremely fit. Meli sneaked little glances at him all during breakfast as if constantly reminding herself of each of his features and comparing them with her memories.

"Do I have egg on my face?" Tor teased as she looked at him again. "Must be syrup on my chin," he decided, wiping his mouth efficiently on a paper napkin.

Bending her head over her plate, she urged him to hurry. She had several things she wanted to show him that day.

"I thought we might take a hike up to the ridge," he said.

She considered the suggestion. "How about doing that tomorrow? We can take a lunch and picnic up at the lookout rock . . . if you like." She left it up to him.

He glanced at her curiously and she knew she was jumpy and indecisive, which was unusual for her. She shivered delicately, wondering what was to come and why she should feel apprehensive about it. After all, she was twenty-nine, old enough to know her own mind and make her own decisions.

"All right," Tor agreed.

After cleaning up the kitchen, they put on padded vests and went for a walk around the camp so Meli could show him what progress had been made since his last tour of inspection.

The dirt road leading to the camp split into a one-lane loop at the camp's entrance. Meli's cabin and the building that was a combination store and gathering place for the guests were inside the loop.

A boat dock with a rental-boat storage building and a bait shop were located at the farthest tip of the loop. On the northeast side of the road were the cabins and camping sites for families; on the southwest, the places for the avid fishermen to set up their tents and campers.

A boat ramp was available to each of these groups, for a creek ran on either side of the camp, their conflux forming another creek that eventually ran into the north fork of the Flathead River.

At a brisk pace, Meli guided Tor around the cabins, which were closed until the summer season, except for the one with the naturalists in it.

"The kids raked pine needles all around," she pointed out. "The needles make an excellent ground cover. They've cleared some of the underbrush and gotten rid of that patch of poison ivy so that children wouldn't get into it."

She was filled with a quiet pride as she indicated the changes and improvements that had been made over the past year. This was her little empire, her niche in the world, and she loved it.

Larch trees, those strange members of the pine

family that dropped their needles each year, were plentiful in the area. She felt an affinity for these trees, which were slightly different from the rest of their kind.

"Come on," she said. "I want to show you what we've done to the store."

Leading the way, she pranced lightly along the road and up the path to the main building, her escort smiling indulgently like a fond parent with an enterprising offspring. She talked in a steady stream—not idle chatter, but an explanation of the progress that had been made.

"As you probably know, cross-country skiing has come into its own. We were booked solid in the cabins from November through March. And this was just our first year! Most of our advertising was word-of-mouth."

Her countenance glowed with health and animation; her eyes flashed as they glanced from the path to his face and then forward to the large, rustic lodge in front of them.

The building was two stories tall, built of massive wooden beams and dressed logs. A huge veranda ran around three sides of it.

"See what we've done to the porch," she bragged, waving an arm in a broad gesture.

The veranda had been enclosed with solid paneling that rose about four feet from the porch and removable screens or shutters that filled in the rest of the space to the roof beams.

Fletcher Robinson saw them approaching and

came down the wide steps with his hand extended in greeting. "Tor! Glad to see you! Come on in, but watch the tools on the steps," he warned. "Good morning, Meli. Did you tell him all about our plans?"

"Not yet. I thought you might like to fill him in," she said, smiling at her manager.

"Actually, a lot of it was Greta's idea. She wanted to start a soup kitchen for the skiers who tromped in half-frozen this winter, but there wasn't room—"

"Until Fletch got the idea of rearranging the store," Meli interrupted.

"Then somebody suggested the porch as a good place to relax in the summer, especially if it was screened against insects, and chairs and tables added so people could sit out here and eat."

It had been three months since Tor had been inside the lodge, and Meli was delighted with the surprise on his face as he looked at the changes the five Robinsons and Meli had accomplished in that time.

Shelves had been built and stacked so that the small store of supplies occupied a sectioned-off alcove from the rest of the large room. Padded benches and chairs built of native timber encircled the massive fireplace at the other end.

Between the store and the fireplace, several tables and chairs had been placed in a casual eating area. A small kitchen had been added along a central wall.

Greta was hovering over the stove, stirring a pot of soup, when the other three came in. Her face, which clearly showed that she had known sorrow in her life, brightened into a happy smile as she put her spoon down and hurried across the room.

"You see," she said to Meli after greeting the younger couple, "the fame of our kitchen has already spread across the country. Are you ready for lunch? Come, I'll fix you a bowl . . ."

The two men laughed. Greta tried to feed everyone who came in. She seemed to think all young people were in imminent danger of starvation if she didn't act at once to get some wholesome food into them.

"We just had breakfast," Tor explained, bringing a split-second pause into the conversation.

Meli rushed into the silence. "Come on down to the dock," she urged. "We have plans there, too."

The dock and bait house were nestled into a groove of land where the smaller creek ran into the larger one. Meli led Tor to the point of land that jutted into the main stream.

"Look, Tor." She pointed toward the opposite side. "If we could get permission to put in a foot-bridge along here and build a garage over there, we could use that old logging road to get to town. That would cut nearly five miles off the trip . . ."

"The road would have to be improved," he noted.

"Yes, I'd like to gravel it or pave it."

He shook his head. "I think that would be beyond your resources. You don't want to overextend your means or move too fast."

"You move fast," she said, reminding him of his business endeavors.

"That's different."

"Why? Because you're a man?" The gentle lines of her face took on a belligerent cast.

His glance was sharply inquiring. "Not particularly. I had other arrows in my quiver. This is your only livelihood."

She shrugged aside his caution. "If I lose it, I can find work. I supported myself for five years before I came back home. And a husband, too," she added.

Tor moved close to her and took her into the warm enclosure of his embrace. "What is it? You're very defensive this weekend. What has happened to upset you?"

His perception startled her.

She wanted to tell him that she needed a change in her life. She wanted to remind him that she was going to be thirty in December, that her life had been static during the past few years.

"Babe?"

Pulling from his arms, she walked quickly away and came to a stop on a jutting rock beside the spring rush of water. The day was rapidly warming and the fresh snow was melting fast.

Her mother had drowned when Meli was eight years old. That, too, had been in the spring with the rivers and lakes swollen with melted snow. They had been visiting in the valley and her mother had taken a boat ride on the lake alone, for she was an early riser and liked to greet the day. The boat had overturned for some unknown reason. Her mother hadn't been able to hold on or make it to shore in the freezing-cold water.

"What are you thinking?" Tor asked quietly as he stopped beside her, not touching but close.

"Of my mother," she replied distantly.

He remained silent.

"She's been dead twenty-one years. My father died two years ago. My marriage officially ended three years ago, although it, too, was dead before that." So many endings, she thought.

For another moment her blue eyes were cloudy with remembrance, and then she smiled, holding out a hand to her waiting companion. "Enough of that. Come on. I'll show you the improvements we've made over on the other side of the camp."

The section of the vacation resort reserved for the avid fishermen was more thickly wooded than the cabin area. The feeling of wilderness was complete; not even the lodge was visible from the campsites.

The three teenagers were throwing very wet snowballs at each other, laughing and shouting like wild creatures. Gretchen saw Tor and Meli first and alerted her brothers.

"Look, it's Meli and San, uh, Mr. Halliday," she said.

Tor's smile was teasingly sardonic. "Santa Claus?" he asked, correctly guessing her first name for him. But there was nothing remotely elfish about him as he stood there in the sun, his hair gleaming like gold and the clarity of his blue eyes rivaling the sky over their heads. He looked as tall and as powerful as a god . . . and as spellbinding.

A lovely blush ran under the smooth skin of the girl. She ducked her head and grinned self-consciously. Meli had the vagrant wish that she were young and starting over in life.

She stayed on the periphery of the group as Tor and the other three discussed the plans for padding the tent sites with pine needles, more for the protection of the tree roots than for the comfort of the campers.

An hour later, she and Tor strolled along the road, heading back to the house.

"You really have been making plans . . . and carrying them out," he added, hearing the hammering coming from the lodge as they approached Meli's cabin.

"Yes." She took a deep breath, thinking that this was the time to tell him of her other plans. Overheating in the afternoon sun, she unzipped her vest and let it flap open in the slight breeze. Tor took her hand and swung it idly between them.

"I've been thinking," he mused aloud before she could make up her mind how to begin.

"About what?" Why that note of trepidation in her voice?

"Us."

Her heart gave a lurch and landed in her throat. She pressed her free hand there as if holding it in.

Tor sat on the top step and pulled her down beside him. He draped a strong arm casually around her shoulders. For a long minute he gazed at the view of forest and trees and water, at the snow which was mostly slush now, and at the signs of civilization creeping into the scene.

"We have an anniversary coming up next month."

He squeezed her shoulders. "Two years. I've never regretted taking time off to come up here on that fishing trip."

She tilted her head at him. "You came up to close a business deal," she said in a pert manner, recovering her equilibrium and her humor.

He gave her a mock scowl. "I could have done that in New York. I came because I needed a break. And I met you."

"Yes," she breathed, suddenly remembering.

"You know, I felt guilty about you for a long time, all the fall and winter, in fact."

Meli was astonished as he actually managed to look guilt-ridden. "What about?"

"Well, I came up for a four-day weekend in May, returned every free moment I could find after that, schemed to get you in my bed, finally succeeded in August, only to find out that your father had recently died and your marriage had fallen through the previous year."

"You thought you had taken advantage of me while I was in a weakened state," she concluded.

"Yes."

She leaned her head on his arm and smiled up at him. "You didn't. My marriage had been over long before that."

"So you said later." His finger traced a line down her forehead, along her short, straight nose and over her lips, coming to rest under her chin while he studied her face with an odd tenderness in his expression. "You married so young."

Lifting her head from his touch, she answered with a wry laugh. "Twenty-one. I thought it was terribly romantic to help my husband get through law school. Boy, I'd not make that mistake again! Talk about being taken to the cleaners!"

Her chuckle was genuine. She no longer felt bitterness or regret over her youthful mistake. It was done with.

"You should have waited until he was established, then sued him for a return on your investment. The courts have been pretty understanding of the woman's side in cases like that."

"I was just glad to get rid of him."

"Then your father died." Tor looked as if he would like to battle the cruelties of fate on her behalf.

Her face went somber. "I was prepared for that. Dad didn't believe in lies or evading the truth. I knew he was ill." She turned to Tor. "I'm glad I came home. My father helped me a lot during those last months. He shared his outlook and his wisdom with me. I got over my hatred of Byron. I accepted my part in the breakup."

"Your part?" he prompted when she was quiet for several seconds.

"Yes. I'm not all that easy to live with. I tend to decide what I'm going to do, then I do it. Poor Byron found it very hard to turn me once I'd started on a course," she stated, giggling.

Tor's laughter was an agreement with her judgment on her personality.

"We're getting off the subject. What I was trying to lead up to was this: What would you like for a present? A real gift, not those silly things I bring you, but something special. What do you want to commemorate our long and happy association?" he asked.

A husband, she thought, and wondered what he would do if she said those very words. He had given her the perfect opening. But she couldn't bring herself to utter the request. She hadn't known she was such a coward! Live and learn, as they say.

"Hey, did you go to sleep?" he demanded, giving her a little shake.

"I'm thinking. I'm thinking," she told him. Standing, she indicated that she was ready to go inside. "I'll let you know when I hit on something."

The telephone rang while they were hanging their vests on the hooks of the lowboy. Tor went to get it. The call was for him, and while he talked, she went into the kitchen to prepare lunch. After laying out steaks for dinner, she made turkey sandwiches, lost in thought as she did.

Already she was realizing how much she would miss Tor. The hours spent walking around the area, the talk with the Robinsons, all combined to remind her how deeply he was woven into the fabric of her life.

Of course, once she met someone and got married, her husband would replace Tor in all ways. More, because he would be with her all the time, either here or wherever they lived. With the Robinsons to manage things, the location of her home would be no problem.

Naturally she was stirred by sadness, but all good things come to an end. Life must move on and so must she. And Tor, too. He was her best friend and she was concerned about his future happiness. It was time he settled down.

He came into the kitchen as she was pouring glasses of cola to go with their sandwiches. Then she placed the food on the table, turned to him, and put her arms around his lean torso.

"I'm glad you came up here on the long weekend too," she said simply, not explaining her sudden desire to say this. Then she pulled away with an abrupt motion. His brow rose in a quizzical arch at her strange action. "Was that the call you were expecting?" she asked.

"Mm-hmm." He sat opposite her and picked up the thick bread slices crowded with wedges of meat. "That merger I was telling you about." He bit off a large bite with strong, white teeth that could nibble without leaving a mark on her delicate skin.

Watching the muscles of his jaw work as he chewed, she felt a longing to take him into her arms, to run her hands over the smooth skin of his broad shoulders, to press her face into the dark gold of his chest hair. A silly impulse. She began to eat, unable to tear her eyes from him.

His fingers were long and supple. He had calluses from tennis and racketball and from the work he often did around the fishing camp. He was skillful at many activities. For her, he had painted, repaired buildings with a hammer and nails, sawed logs . . . and made love, oh so many times.

Sensations shivered down her back and across her breasts as if his hands were caressing her at that moment. He had only to look at her for her passion to flare into urgent desire. And he seemed to react in the same way to her.

She looked at his mouth as he took another bite and ate hungrily, as intent on that task as he was on every task he undertook. His lips sometimes looked hard, uncompromising, but there was a whimsical touch of humor around his eyes and in the way he quirked his right brow. He had kissed her a million times, all over.

Did she really want to give that up? Could she? A precognition of the barrenness of life without Tor came to her. Maybe she wouldn't have to give him up—not entirely. Then she would have her husband and her best friend too. Some of her father's optimism surged within her, bringing a smile in its wake. She would have what she wanted from life or else!

"I think you're interested in more than food," he teased with a throaty chuckle that brought unexpected heat to her face.

"Have you decided what to do with Mr. Grainger?" she asked to distract him from her glowing face.

Tor had recently been working on merging two subsidiaries of his conglomerate into one autonomous company. Each subsidiary had its own general manager and one of them was going to have to go. That was the problem. Tor wanted to make the younger manager president of the new company.

Tor took a long gulp of cola before shaking his head. "Not yet. I still don't want to put him under the other man, but I don't really have another position for him."

· "Have you asked him how he would feel about it? Maybe he'd rather be a vice-president. Maybe he doesn't want to have responsibility for the larger company."

His smile flashed over her. "No man wants to take second place after sitting in the number one chair," he said, explaining the male psyche to her.

Meli disagreed. "You don't know that. You're speaking for yourself. You'd probably go out and start a new company if you couldn't be top dog, but not everyone is like that."

"Oh, is that right?" Amusement glittered in the depths of his eyes, appeared in the lift of his brow as he teased her with his question.

"Yes," she said, wrinkling her nose in a saucy fashion at him. She finished her meal, wiped her mouth prettily, and carried her dishes to the sink. Leaning against the counter, she stared out the window, but all her senses were tuned to the man behind her, still at the table. The shadows of afternoon were growing long, she noted. Soon it would be night.

"Are you going back tomorrow?" she asked.

"No," he replied. "I meant to tell you and forgot.

That call was from Betty. She said she was able to put off a Monday meeting until Tuesday, so I'll have an extra day."

Meli had spoken to Tor's secretary several times. He described her as being efficient, pleasant, and middle-aged, but Meli thought the woman sounded young over the telephone . . . and very pleasant.

The chair legs scraped on the floor. Tor brought his dishes over, then slipped his arms around Meli. After several bites on her neck, he murmured, "Thanks for dessert."

"Vampire." She shied away from him as if frightened.

He came after her as she dashed into the living room and ran in a circle around the sofa. He caught her by the simple expedient of vaulting over the obstruction.

A long moment later, when he lifted his mouth from hers, she said, "Let's build a fire. It's getting cold in here."

With a show of reluctance, he let her go and went to the fireplace. He took newspaper and kindling from the woodbox, arranged it expertly in the grate, and struck a match to it. When the flames licked merrily over the small pieces of wood, he added larger pieces, then the back log, which would burn most of the night.

Bowing from the waist at Meli, who sat cross-legged on the oval braided rug, he inquired if she had any further orders.

"Will you grill steaks in the fire tonight for dinner?"

"Yes. Anything else?" His smile was lazy, filled with a sort of waiting amusement. He would make his own requests when the time was right, it seemed to say.

She hesitated. "No, that's all."

A frown replaced the smile. His face registered disbelief. "Sure?" he questioned, studying her face.

"Mm-hmm." She rose to her knees to poke the fire, hiding her face with the forward sweep of her hair.

"Hey, leave my fire alone!" he ordered, indignant that she would dare touch his masterpiece. He removed the poker from her hand and fixed the logs to suit himself, nodding complacently when he had them back in place. "There!" he said.

While he stretched out on the sofa for a nap, she read a book she had started the night before. After finishing that, she sat and stared into the fire as night softly enfolded the cabin.

Although she considered herself a morning person, this was the time of day she liked the best, especially when Tor was with her. When night drew its curtains on the world, shutting them into the snug security of the cabin, she was pierced with a sweet peace and a sense of purpose in being, in just existing.

With a deep sigh, she wished her life could stay this way. In the same moment she knew she was lying. She was ready to move on. She rose and went to the kitchen, washed some potatoes, oiled and wrapped them in foil, and then returned to the living room to tuck them into the hot ashes of the fire.

Next she rubbed seasoning into the two steaks. Fortunately she and Greta had gone to the grocery before the snow; therefore, she had fresh vegetables to make a salad. After taking care of that, she returned to her place on the rug, her back against the sofa seat.

Tor's arm curved around her, coming down over her right shoulder and deftly penetrating the vee opening of her plaid shirt. Through the blue knit, he caressed her left breast until the nipple responded and her breath was coming raggedly from her throat.

"Come here," he murmured, sliding down on the couch until his face was at the edge. She turned her head to meet his lips. His hands on her arms turned her body to deepen the embrace. For a long time he kissed her, his lips toying with hers, his tongue intimate in her mouth. Both pairs of eyes were smoky with passion by the time he released her.

Working together, they finished preparing the meal she had started. He easily followed her orders and she marveled over that, in light of what he had said about being number one. She realized that she sometimes followed his commands and he sometimes followed hers, it didn't seem to matter which, and they had never argued over who was going to be boss at a particular time.

Later, over brandy, they sat on the rug and watched the flames hiss and leap. His arm rested on the sofa cushions behind her and his fingers were on her collarbone, rubbing absently until she trapped them between cheek and raised shoulder.

Chuckling, he set his glass aside and pulled her into his arms, eager to fulfill the earlier promise of his kisses. "Babe, babe," he muttered almost under his breath, his voice hoarse with yearning.

He touched her breasts in tender, fierce forays designed to leave her in no doubt of his intent and to encourage her to surrender. She shivered with passionate delight, her fingers stroking through his blond hair before roving down his neck, his shoulders, and finally tugging at his shirt, wanting it out of her way as she explored.

Moving them apart, he removed both the tawny gold shirt and the T-shirt; then he did the same for her, taking off her outer shirt and the knit turtleneck. Chills raced across her skin, drawing soft laughter from him.

"I'll soon have you warm again," he whispered. Leaning against the sofa seat, he held her against his chest after setting her across his hard thighs. His beard lightly sanded her chin as his lips found hers again.

She wrapped her arms tightly around him, controlling her passion, willing it to rise slowly, to last as he liked it to. She was always greedy, wanting it all right away.

"It's all right," he assured her. His hands swept down her smooth back. "We'll do it the way you like this time."

Carefully, he levered them to the floor, the braided rug protecting their bare skin. His hand went to the snap of her jeans, unfastened it and the zipper.

He peeled the material over her hips and down her legs and tossed them aside. He left her socks on, knowing she hated cold feet.

The rest of his clothing joined hers, and then he was stretching his splendid golden length beside the winter paleness of her slender body. Tension began to coil in her lower abdomen until she was near the breaking point. His caresses grew more and more intimate on her thighs while his lips searched out all the sensitive places from her temples to her breasts, along her ribs to the curve of her groin, finally joining the meandering paths of his hands.

"Tor!" she cried urgently, arching her hips to his touch, wanting more and more from him. He was a generous lover, and he gave her everything she wanted.

"Yes, darling, yes." He coaxed the full response from her, anticipating her every move like a partner in a ballet of fierce emotion, a dance of fire.

She writhed beside him, stroking him with the slippery curves of her glowing body. Holding himself back, he brought her to rapture and then joined her. She sobbed helplessly in his arms.

"Oh, Tor," she moaned later as he again lay beside her.

"Shall we establish a new record?" he asked, a gleam of challenge in the cobalt eyes which still burned with hunger.

She shook her head weakly. "No marathon tonight, please," she pleaded, a smile flitting over her reddened lips.

His laughter strayed across her breast as he began the ritual dance once more. "Is this good?" he asked. "Is this?" His mouth closed with sensual skill over one breast, and his large hand massaged the other as fire burst from the embers to consume her with the old-new need for him.

"You're like silk and fire," he exclaimed, running his hands down her sides. "Hot, so hot . . ."

His tongue stabbed in circling spirals along the pale pink aureole. She was flaming, flaming for him. She moved passionately against him, eliciting a gasp that he could no longer withhold.

Quickly, he raised himself over her, bringing them together with masculine grace. "Babe," he groaned, "babe," needing her now as much as she needed him.

Her eyes, heavy-lidded, watched as he surged within the embrace of her body. His lean form reflected the firelight in the sheen of perspiration that covered him. He was beautiful, radiant, his skin overlaid in pinks and golds like the dawn, as her own was, she saw. They were lovely together, like the finger rays of the sun against the dawning sky.

"Tor!" she cried. "Tor! Darling!" Then, "Oh, love," quietly as they came to rest, he still nestled in the cradle of her warm body.

Later, after a shower, they slipped on their pajamas and ate brownies and milk in front of the fire. It came to her that they mostly ate, slept, and made love when they were together, the most basic and elemental of human acts of sharing.

"You didn't answer my question," he reminded her in the husky tones of a contented mountain cat.

She yawned, answering with her own question in the middle of it. "What?"

"What do you want for an anniversary gift?"

"I want a husband," she said.

Chapter Three

She couldn't believe she had blurted out her plans that way. What would Tor think?

Glancing sideways at him, expecting to find him mocking or angry, she found instead that he was thoughtful.

Raising one knee, he propped his forearm across it and stared into the leaping, dancing flames. He looked like a golden cougar, brooding and unpredictable.

At last he nodded. "It's the Robinsons, isn't it?" he inquired softly, his voice a deep rumble in his chest. "I knew something was bothering you. And has been for a long time."

"The Robinsons?" Meli echoed the name without comprehension. What did they have to do with anything?

"Yes, their censure . . ."

She shook her head. "They have no authority over me. How can they censure what I do?" She frowned. What in the world had put him on this train of thought?

"Come on, babe! Don't try to fool me." His glance was impatient. His brows lowered dangerously.

"I'm not trying to fool you. I just don't know what you're talking about. What do the Robinsons have to do with my decision to get married again?"

She stared while he jumped lightly to his feet to take a couple of turns around the room. She decided he didn't look dangerous, only troubled. This reaction confused her all the more. Expecting laughter or anger, she didn't understand what was troubling him.

Of course! He must be realizing the implications her marriage held for their future . . . or rather, lack of one. He knew he couldn't remain her lover when she took a husband. But she had thought he would be angry because of that, not strangely meditative, as he appeared to be, pacing the length of the room and back.

He flopped down on the hearth rug again. "Do you think I didn't get the significance of that little pause that you leaped to fill when I said we had just had breakfast? Naturally Fletch and Greta assumed —correctly—that we had only recently gotten up and that we had slept together."

"I don't care—" she began.

"And then there were Gretchen's remarks about Santa Claus, your drop-in-from-the-blue boyfriend."

The muscles of his jaws worked as if he were gnashing his teeth together. Meli was fascinated by the action, staring until she realized he was waiting for some reaction from her. She cleared her throat, thinking about tactful ways to proceed before she answered. He had gone over the boundary of introspection into annoyance. It wouldn't take much more to send him into a real temper.

"I don't mind her teasing. It's all done in good-natured fun, nothing malicious. Honestly, my decision had nothing to do with the Robinsons or their opinion of my personal affairs," she declared firmly.

"I recognize a case of middle-class morality when I see one," he scoffed, finally coming to a reaction she could definitely recognize.

"You're wrong," she said quietly, firmly. "This was my own conclusion, based on an assessment of my own life and my future. I want something more, or at least different, than what I now have." Her gaze at him was defiant.

A large, caressing hand slipped behind her neck, cupping it gently. Tor's long fingers rubbed the tense muscles there for a long minute. Looking into the compassionate depths of his eyes, she was slightly disconcerted. He felt sorry for her?

"Babe, babe," he murmured, his voice like a sigh on a snow-chilled breeze. "Marriage won't give you what you want. Believe me . . ."

She jerked away from his hand. "Why should I believe you? You've never been married."

"And you have," he reminded her harshly. "Didn't you learn anything from it?"

Taken aback by his return attack, she was speechless. But only for a second. "Of course I did! But that has nothing to do with now. I'm twenty-nine years old, not twenty-one. I should hope I've matured considerably since then."

"Then act like it," he snapped, his brows jerking together above his nose.

Gone were all her logical arguments, her hopes for a quiet, controlled presentation of her views in case he gave her a hard time about her plans. "Why, why, you arrogant . . . you overbearing . . ." she spluttered, casting about in her chaotic thoughts for a name to describe him and his superior attitude. She thought of it. "Chauvinist!"

Rising to her knees, she glared down on him. He glared back, then grabbed her wrists and gave her a little shake.

"You don't know what you're talking about," he gritted softly at her. "And don't resort to name-calling. It doesn't get you anywhere."

"Then stop implying I'm a baby and incapable of knowing my own wants!" She pulled her arms free and sat back on her heels, her mouth compressed insolently.

Tor ran a hand through his hair, his chest heaving in a heartfelt sigh. She wasn't moved by it.

"Look, Meli," he said, deciding to reason with her. "I understand, really I do. You're going to be thirty on your next birthday and you feel you're maybe missing something, that life is getting away from you . . ." He paused, raising an inquiring brow at her to ask if he was on the right track.

Meli smiled in relief. She clasped her hands together in her lap. "Yes, that's part of it."

His large hand covered both of hers. "I thought so." He smiled sadly. "But marriage isn't the answer. Wait a minute," he requested as she clouded into a frown again.

"What for? So you can lecture me some more?" But she quieted as his hand pressed hers.

For a long while he was silent as he gathered his thoughts. Then, "I've seen marriage for money and for love. Neither works. I knew a long time before my parents broke up that my mother married my father for his money. I watched their marriage fall apart and my dad become bitter when Mother met someone else."

Meli's gentle heart was stricken as she listened to Tor explain the sad, intimate details of his youth to her. "Tor, I'm sorry," she whispered.

He shook his head. "That's not all of it. My mother's second husband gave her a miserable life. She had fallen in love with a cheat." His bark of laughter was acid. "She should have known that a man who would play around with a married woman would have no conscience about playing around on a wife of his own."

"Is that why she divorced him?"

"Yes, she stood it as long as she could, then she left. It seemed to take all the will to live out of her.

She didn't commit suicide, but gradually her spirit broke. One winter she caught the flu, then pneumonia. And she died," he said with heavy finality.

"I'm so terribly sorry," Meli repeated, seeing the destruction of his family life in the skeletal outline.

Quietly, because he was lost in his reflections, she gathered up the brownie plates and milk glasses and took them to the kitchen. She squirted a little detergent on a sponge and washed up the items, then put them on the drainrack to dry.

Poor Tor. It was the first time he had disclosed so much of his early life to her, although she had had hints that not all had been well during his growing years. She could understand his bitterness toward marriage, but she wasn't going to let it color her outlook on life. She wondered if, emotionally, he wasn't trapped in his unhappy adolescence.

She returned to the living room and sat down gracefully on the rug again, resting her head on the sofa seat, her eyes intent on the fire.

When Tor slipped an arm around her and pulled her head to his shoulder, she smiled up at him lovingly. His lips bestowed a patchwork of kisses on hers, tickling at the corners with the tip of his tongue.

"Your breath smells of chocolate," he accused playfully, once more in a teasing humor.

"So does yours," she retorted. She licked and then tasted experimentally along his mouth. "And of walnuts."

He cupped the side of her face with his free hand,

holding her head ready for his kiss; then he slid his fingers into her hair as his mouth connected with hers in a devouring kiss that left them both hungry for more of each other. The passionate determination that was part of the very essence of him touched her deeply, claiming her attention in this most elemental way that was, at the same time, much more than merely physical.

There was something very basic between them, she acknowledged; something more than passion had brought him to her for two years. It was too difficult to get here, and there were too many other women available to him for their relationship to have lasted this long without being much more than physical. For a soul-stirring moment, she wished . . . she wished . . .

She tossed off the sudden yearning. She dealt in realities; the reality was that it was time to move on. The heat from his body as he embraced her reduced all thoughts to shreds and then made them disappear altogether.

"Tor," she whispered in wonder as his hands slipped under her pajamas and caressed her back.

"Do you like this?" he asked on a note of teasing laughter. He was touching her breasts gently

"Yes," she gasped, catching his shoulders to keep from melting against him like a candle before the fire. He continued to tease and coax her small breasts.

"You're a glutton for punishment, woman," he growled against her cheek. "Or I am."

Laughing softly, Meli ran her hands down his chest, stopping to rub his nipples in tiny circles until they were as contracted as her own.

"Shall we go to bed?" he inquired, nibbling on her earlobe.

"Yes," she hissed, drawing out the sound while her tongue traced the outer edge of his ear.

"Witch," he rebuked her, pulling away. They turned out the lights and went up the stairs.

In bed with the light out, he held her fast in the curving spoon of his body, her back to his chest. Each of them was content to go to sleep, knowing they had two more days to finish the love play they had started downstairs in front of the fire.

"See?" he asked sleepily. "Isn't this the best? We have it all, everything a person could want, right now. Why clutter up life with marriage? Right?"

"No," she disagreed, her body tensing in his embrace. "I still want to get married."

He sat up abruptly and reached across her to turn on the lamp. His chest gleamed a smooth, even tan in the soft light, each golden hair glinting as if it had gold dust sprinkled on it.

"Damn it, Meli, we just went over this ridiculous notion of yours. Why ruin a perfect relationship with something as antiquated as marriage!"

She plumped up the pillows and threw herself back on them against the headboard. Her arms were crossed angrily in front of her like a barrier. "It's not ridiculous!" she stated.

"The hell it isn't!"

They exchanged glares like ancient enemies meet-

ing accidentally at the house of a mutual acquaintance.

"Look," he began.

"No!" She refused to listen.

"You pigheaded little moron!"

"Names, Tor, will get you nothing . . . except a
fast ticket back to Georgia!" She smiled through her
teeth at him.

Chillbumps made an interesting texture on his
bare skin as the cool air of the bedroom penetrated
the aura of warmth around him. Grumbling, he
searched around on the floor until he found his
pajama top and tugged it on. He turned to face her,
intent on convincing her of the merit of his argument.

She waved an insolent hand at him. "I don't care
what you say. Nothing will change my mind. I want
to get married and that's that!"

His blade of a nose almost touched hers as he
leaned forward. "Is that right?" he drawled. "And
what about my wants? What if I just out-and-out
refuse?" he demanded triumphantly.

Meli looked completely blank. "Refuse what?"
she asked, confused.

"To marry you," he retorted.

Her mouth dropped open.

"Ha!" He pounced on her stupefaction. "You
didn't think of that, did you?" He practically rubbed
his hands together in glee at having gotten the best
of her. "Marriage has never been a part of my plans.
I like my life just as it is!"

"Oh, Tor," Meli choked. "Oh, Tor." For a minute

that was all she could say. Memories of their first summer, of the resurgence of that overpowering emotion—she had thought it was love at the time— crowded into her mind. For a brief time that summer she had thought they would marry. Closing the door on that reminiscence, she smiled gently at him. "I never meant I was going to marry you," she explained.

After a second of total confusion on his part, a flush spread up his face. "Who, then, did you mean?" he demanded angrily. He jerked away when she instinctively reached out to comfort him. "Answer me!" he gritted.

"I'm sorry, Tor," she apologized. "Really, it didn't occur to me that you would think I meant you."

"That's obvious," he said, his voice dry and his face stern. He had himself under tight control. "Perhaps you would tell me just what you have in mind? You've met someone . . ."

"No, nothing like that." She paused, then added, "I wouldn't sleep with one man if I had met another that I wanted to get involved with. Did you think I would?"

"How should I know what women will do when they get one of their crazy notions?" At her look of reproach, he paused. "I'm sorry. I didn't mean that."

"That's okay," she said softly. "I guess I dealt you a greater shock than I realized. I thought you really did understand when you said you did."

He stood and pulled on his pajama bottoms.

Apparently he thought he had regained his dignity
with this act, because he assumed a look of wisdom
as he sat on the side of the bed and, like a forgiving
father, asked to hear her story.

"There's no story. It's just that I've been thinking
for a long while about the empty places in my life.
Now I've decided I want them filled . . . with a
husband. That's where you can help."

"Me?" he asked, half in protest, half in humor.

"Yes. You know so many people, I'm sure you
must know someone just right for me."

Meli smiled brilliantly at her shocked lover as she
waited for him to name several candidates.

"Let me get this straight. You want *me* to help *you*
find a husband? I wonder if Ann Landers ever had a
case like this," he mused in disbelief after Meli
nodded vigorously. "You have got to be kidding."

"No, I'm not, Tor. And if you won't help me, I'll
just have to look on my own. Although it would save
me a lot of time if you could introduce me to some
eligible men. You know my tastes so well."

"I can't believe this," he said.

"Why not?" she asked very innocently.

His eyes narrowed, and this time "dangerous" was
the correct description. "All right, Meli, who is he?
Someone who came up here on a fishing trip?"

She realized with a shock—and a forgivable feminine thrill—that Tor was jealous. Could it be that he
was more involved with her than she thought? No, it
was just normal male possessive jealousy, she decided. "There's no one else," she said.

"You want to break it off with me, don't you? Is

this your way of leading up to it, of breaking it to me gently? Don't lie," he warned her fiercely.

"I'm not lying," she said. "You and Byron have been the only—"

"I'm not letting you go," he said as if she hadn't spoken a word. "No telling what kind of person you'll get mixed up with. You'll only be hurt again, and I'll be damned if I'll let you do it." His hands closed on her shoulders. "I'm not going to stand by and see you hurt again because of some harebrained idea you hatched up here by yourself this winter. You've let yourself get in a tizzy about getting old," he decided.

Meli tried to disagree but he wouldn't have it.

"You're not getting old, honey. You're more beautiful each time I see you and that's the honest-to-God truth. You probably were lonesome the past few months, but I'll come up more often, I promise. You'll snap out of this in no time," he assured her.

He looked so pleased with this bit of masculine logic that she was swamped by tenderness for him. She hugged him to her and felt the relaxing of his tense frame.

"Oh, Tor, you're so precious, too precious for words," she exclaimed. "And you're the only lover I've ever had, not counting Byron." Her marriage had been nothing like the relationship she shared with this golden lion.

His hands went to his buttons. "Good. Now that we've gotten this straightened out, let's get some sleep."

She watched, smiling, as he threw off his pajamas

again. Tomorrow would be time enough to straighten him out, she thought, settling against his chest when he was once again in bed and the light was out. She yawned sleepily. "Good night, Tor."

"Good night, sweetheart," he said, going promptly to sleep.

Meli puttered quietly about the kitchen on Sunday morning. The Robinson kids had gone out to get the Sunday paper at the end of the road and had brought hers to her cabin. It was neatly folded on one side of the table.

She was making gravy the way Tor liked it, to go over the biscuits that were baking in the oven. A platter of bacon and eggs was ready on the back of the stove.

"Tor!" she yelled. "Breakfast."

By the time she had placed their plates and the food on the table, poured coffee and prepared orange juice, he came into the room, sniffing appreciatively. "I'm hungry. That looks delicious."

He kissed her cheek, patted her rump, and then took his place after she sat down. He looked exactly like a huge mountain cat that was perfectly happy with its life, she noted.

His gleaming hair shone like metal in the flood of sunlight through the kitchen window. Her own was a deeper hue of the same color.

"Looks like a good day for our hike. Have you been outside?" he asked, breaking open a hot biscuit and spooning the gravy over it.

She fixed her biscuit like his, and chopped her egg

into bits to eat with it. She raised her smoky blue
eyes to find him watching her with a curious expression on his face. "It's lovely outside. Brisk right
now, but it will be a lot warmer by noon. The snow
will be gone by then, too, except under the trees on
the north side of the slopes. It'll be nice up on
Lookout Point."

"Let's hurry then."

He ate with relish, enjoying the good things of his
life with a gusto that was natural and uninhibited. If
things went wrong, he acted at once to right them,
certain in his own mind about the way they ought to
be. His enjoyment of life and his determination were
two of the things that had attracted Meli to him from
the first.

While he washed the dishes, she went upstairs and
dressed in comfortable pants and a shirt and put on
her lightweight trail shoes, which she found better
for hiking than her boots. In a few minutes she
returned, and together they packed lunches, slipped
into windbreakers and padded vests and were off.
Meli always experienced a sense of adventure when
she went off like this with Tor.

She glanced at his strong profile as he backed the
Jeep out of her drive and started along the loop.
They would drive to a spot at the base of a long,
spiny ridge, then walk up the sloping mountain to
Lookout Point.

His dark blue eyes met hers as he swung the
vehicle into the long, slow arc of the curving road.
His smile was thoughtful rather than carefree this
morning.

Meli considered Tor a man of action who was not particularly given to introspection, yet here he was again, engrossed in his thoughts. She wondered why. Had her talk about marriage brought the subject to his mind? Her heart knocked painfully against her ribs. Maybe marriage wasn't a part of his plans, but it was still very much a part of hers. He was just going to have to accept that fact.

"Friday night," he said, "when I was driving up here, I kept visualizing how it would be when I arrived. In my mind, I could see you curled up in bed, all snug in your nightgown, and I wished I could sneak into the house and climb in bed with you without your knowing I was within a thousand miles of here."

She roused from her musing to gaze at him with inquiring eyes. "Why?"

"I wanted you to wake up when I started making love to you, not before. But I figured I would have to stand on the porch, pounding on the door to wake you up . . ."

"And I would get up and let you in, all grumpy for being woken up," she said, giggling.

His grin of acknowledgment was brief. With a strange seriousness, he continued, "But when I came around the bend of the road, there was the cabin, its windows spilling light out over the snow like beacons lit just for me."

"But I really didn't expect you," she murmured, wondering now if she hadn't subconsciously thought he might come and that was why she hadn't felt sleepy.

"When you opened the door, you were framed in light," he said. "The scene looked like one of those pictures done in pencil or charcoal."

"Chiaroscuro." At his raised brow, she explained, "A study in light and shadow." It was a new word, recently learned from a trip to New York's many art galleries.

A blob of wet, icy snow hit the windshield. Sam and Troy pelted the vehicle with several more snowballs as the road curved into the edge of the woods at the point where the loop became one road again. Meli waved goodbye over her shoulder.

"Crazy kids," Tor said good-naturedly as he speeded up.

Except for patches under the thickest covering of trees, the snow was mostly gone from the gravel road now and they could make better time. They lapsed into companionable silence for the remainder of the trip, the old comfort of being together restored by the peace and beauty around them.

An hour later, Tor pulled the Jeep to the side of the rough road and parked. Hoisting the knapsack onto his back, he and Meli started off through the woods, following a faint trail toward the eastern crest of a high ridge.

Their passage was marked only by birdcalls or the scolding of a squirrel in the branches of the evergreens. Ponderosa pines, Douglas fir, and larch raised a lofty canopy over their heads. In the brief summer, beargrass, Indian paintbrush, fireweed, and asters would add brilliant color in the valleys.

Myriad mountain streams ran off the slopes down into the water- and glacier-eroded valley to join the north fork of the Flathead River.

Meli drew a deep breath of the chilly air. She could hear the steady beat of her heart deep inside and wished she could stay out here forever.

Alone, or with Tor?

She watched the movements of his body as he led the way up the increasingly harder trail. Life was more fun with a friend, she admitted. She would bring her husband here when she married.

It was almost twelve o'clock when they stepped over the last piece of fallen log, climbed the last rocky steep, and emerged on the flat ridge of rock called Lookout Point by the local residents.

At this spot, a view that could make the most mundane heart sing opened along the valley. Immediately below the jutting point of rock, the land was scooped into a natural amphitheater, a glacial cirque, while further to the north, a knifelike crest called an arête thrust above the treetops. The floor of an ancient sea had been pushed up and sculpted by nature into majestic peaks and hollows. Meli thought there could be no place on earth more beautiful.

"Beautiful, isn't it?" Tor spoke her thoughts aloud. He dropped the backpack to the hard surface and walked over to the edge, joining her as she eagerly searched out all her favorite sights.

"Canada," she murmured, looking to her left. There was no noticeable difference at the point where one country ended and another began. It was all mountains, stretching away seemingly to infinity.

Tor gave her a singularly expressive look before dropping Indian-fashion to the ground. "Let's eat while we admire the scene." He opened the knapsack and laid out their lunch.

She sat opposite him, accepted a plastic cup of steaming coffee, and sipped it while she continued gazing across the valley. Absently she took the sandwich he unwrapped and handed to her.

"You'd miss this if you left," he told her.

"It would always be here, waiting for my return." A sharp note of contradiction entered her soft tones. "Have you ever been over the Going-to-the-Sun road that crosses the park?"

"No. Why?"

"It would make a lovely place to honeymoon," she said, thinking of the park in general with its acres of privacy. She knew of a place next to a creek that had only seven campsites.

From the corner of her eye, she saw his hand jerk, sloshing his coffee. A low curse followed the action.

"I thought we got that idea squared away last night," he snapped at her after mopping his damp hand on his handkerchief.

"You may have thought that; I didn't," she responded equably. "That is, I've known for some time what I was going to do. Now it's simply a matter of convincing you that I mean business." She grinned impishly at his obvious chagrin.

"Did anybody ever tell you that you have a one-track mind?" he demanded.

She nodded her head, her grin spreading into a derisive smile. "My ex-husband used to mention it often near the end of our marriage. The poor guy never got over the shock of my refusing to go to another cocktail party after years of hanging on every word he said."

Tor latched on to her confession. "You see? Sooner or later the thrill of playing house wears off and then you get on each other's nerves."

"You may be right," she agreed, laughing about his view of marriage and refusing to take his advice seriously. "But it was my fault in the first place. Now I'm much wiser."

He was openly skeptical. "How's that?" he drawled. He munched on a dill pickle, managing to look distantly superior and interested all at the same time.

"Well, you know I went to school in the valley with the same kids from first grade to graduation. When I went off to college, it was like a whole new world. I took one look at Byron with those blue eyes and that black hair and *flipped* over him! He didn't stand a chance once I'd made up my mind that he was the one. And he thought it was a good deal too, after he found out I had some money from my mother's insurance. Between that and my job in the registrar's office, we lived pretty well."

"I'd say he had it made," Tor butted in.

"Yes, he got through law school without having to work. His family couldn't help him financially, so I came in handy."

Tor's eyes darkened. "You don't sound it, but you must be bitter. Any normal person would be."

"I was at first when I realized just how I'd been used, but later, well, I was just glad to be out of it. He wasn't the person I had thought he was; I wasn't the society hostess he wanted for a wife. It was a mutual parting of the ways." She shrugged philosophically.

"And now you want to repeat that error," he reminded her, mockery in his deep voice.

The breeze blew a strand of hair across her face. She tucked it behind her ear. She thought about his statement, and for a moment she was scared that she would repeat past mistakes. The fear summoned up anger about his lack of understanding.

"I'll be more careful this time," she said stiffly. "I know what I want in a man—maturity, a sense of humor, self-confidence. I want a man who accepts himself as a person, who likes himself, and who will not feel threatened by the same qualities in me."

Tor stuffed the sandwich wrappers and cups back into the bag, closed it and laid it aside. He moved over to her so that their shoulders were touching, making her conscious of him in a physical way.

She was aware of him as she had been of no other man, not even Byron, who had been her first great romance. Tor was a much better lover, perceptive and considerate in a way that her ex-husband had not been capable of. Little eddies of warmth began to stir in her blood, increasing as she saw his gaze on her.

"And where are you going to find this ideal man?" he asked huskily, his eyes narrowing to sexy slits as he studied her gentle features and heightened color. He knew she was responding as she always did to his slightest advance. His lazy smile was pure anticipation.

"I told you I needed your help. But if you won't give it, I'll manage on my own." She turned her face from his knowing gaze, her lips sealed together.

"How will you manage?" His breath touched the side of her cheek, blew against her ear, causing a shiver to cascade down her neck. She began to feel hot and unfastened her vest. Tor removed it for her, then took off his own. They slipped out of their jackets and put them aside.

"I'll go to New York . . ."

"New York!" The wind picked up the word and brought it back to them in a faint echo. "You don't know anything about New York. You'd get lost . . . and mugged!"

Her spine went as straight as a ramrod. "I know New York quite well, for your information. I went there three times this past winter. And to Chicago once."

One dark brow rose to meet the golden lock that tumbled on his forehead. "When? What for?"

"To see some shows and visit some art galleries and museums," she replied defiantly.

More than anything else, her trips had brought home to her the fact of her single status. She had been uncomfortable traveling on her own in a world made for couples. That had been one more factor in her determination to find someone of her own to share her life with.

"Why didn't you call me?" he demanded. "I have an apartment in New York . . . as you know. You could have stayed in it, saved your money and—"

"I can afford to pay my own way!" She was affronted by his suggestion.

His expression lightened as he looked at her proud bearing. "I know you wouldn't do anything you couldn't afford, especially for entertainment. I meant you could have stayed longer, gone to more shows for the same amount of money. If you didn't want me along, you could have said so. I wouldn't have bothered you."

Meli stared at him in amazement. Could the pain she saw in his eyes be real? Had she hurt his feelings by not telling him of her plans and by going on her own? She hadn't wanted to intrude in his life. After all, he had never invited her to visit him even though he had felt quite free to drop in on her without notice. But men were like that, she thought. They liked roughing it once in a while, something for a change of pace.

How flattering, she thought wryly to herself, to be a change of pace. From Mary Beth? Or people like her, she decided. Not as lovers, but as friends. She still held the notion that he had no other women.

She became confused as she contemplated his expression, catching him in a moment of vulnerability, it seemed.

She touched his arm lightly. "Would you have wanted me?" she asked, unsure of his true feelings.

"Yes," he said. "Did you think I wouldn't?"

"I . . . I didn't know. You've never invited me before."

He looked as if he couldn't believe what he had just heard. "Invited! Since when have we needed invitations between us? Aren't we lovers? Doesn't that give us rights in each other's lives?"

"Does it?" She wasn't going to take anything for granted.

"Of course it does!" he protested. "I thought you didn't want to come. You always seemed so happy here in the camp, as if you didn't really need anything else. In two years, you've never dropped in to surprise me with a visit," he said softly, almost accusingly.

Meli's heart was beating very fast at this disclosure. Now she was positive there had been no other women in his life. The smile she turned on him was real. "Our planes would have probably crossed in midair, you on your way here, me on my way there."

His chuckle indicated his agreement. His arm went around her waist and his lips nuzzled below her ear. "Listen, I was planning on coming up for a long weekend at the end of the month. Why don't you come visit me instead? I'll meet you in New York. We can take in some shows or whatever you like."

She listened attentively, a tiny smile resting in the corner of her mouth. When he finished, she shook her head. "Thank you anyway, but no," she said.

"What do you mean, no?" he gritted at her.

"No. N-O. No. I have other plans." There was half a note of regret in her voice. He had made it sound so enticing.

"Husband-hunting?" he asked in scathing tones.

She grinned. "Exactly."

Chapter Four

The battle raged between them during the entire return trip to the fishing camp. Silently. Tor hardly spoke a word to her, and those that were necessary were harshly critical.

When he parked the Jeep, he climbed out, handed her the empty backpack and stalked off across the road in the direction of the creek. Meli carried the bag into the cabin to dispose of their trash and wash the thermos before storing the items again. After finishing the chore, she went outside and sat on the front porch to wait for her angry lover to return.

She had expected a show of resistance on his part . . . and had gotten it, she thought ruefully. Well, he was just going to have to accept the change in the status quo. It would be no problem for him to find another woman to take her place.

A little knot of pain formed in her heart and she had to admit that she, too, hated to end her relationship with her golden lover. Would she be able to find another man who was a wonderful friend and a thrilling partner, all in one handsome package?

She went into the cabin and put on a pot of chili to simmer. After taking dough out of the refrigerator, she set it aside to rise in a loaf pan, then went into the living room to prepare the fireplace for a fire later in the day. Finished, she lay down on the couch and closed her eyes, thinking she would rest while waiting for Tor's return.

It was a couple of hours later when she woke up. The shadows of twilight darkened the windows. The fire was burning with soothing cheer, murmuring to itself as it leaped and danced in the hearth. The smell of baking bread filled the air and brought forth a low growl from her stomach.

Tor came to the living room doorway. "Supper," he announced. He grinned at her round-eyed surprise.

Meli washed up in the downstairs bathroom before going to the kitchen for the meal. Combing her hair, she decided that Tor was probably confident he could charm her out of her weird notion. But she was prepared for him.

"How pretty," she commented a few minutes later, surveying the table setting.

He had placed several sprays of greenery in a squat vase and lit two candles on either side of his centerpiece. The fresh loaf of bread was on a cutting board beside a pot of honey and a dish of butter.

Large bowls of chili with cheese melting on top waited at each place. He held her chair for her.

"Anything to please the lady." He was being very gallant. Meli almost laughed at his obvious tactics.

"Including finding a husband for her?" she quipped under her breath.

His face darkened but he held his tongue. He was as charming during the meal as she had expected, speaking of past hiking and camping trips, reminding her of the pleasures of past experiences that they had shared.

He wiped the honey off her fingers with a damp paper towel when she finished eating and shooed her into the living room while he took care of the dishes.

She made a face and grinned to herself as she dropped to the rug in front of the fireplace. In a short time, Tor came out and joined her on the rug, rolling his sleeves down his arms but not buttoning the cuffs. His arms immediately went around her, hauling her across his lap. His lips covered hers in an instant attack that took her completely by surprise.

At first she tried to withhold herself from the embrace, but as always, she soon started to melt. There was no way to wean herself gradually from this intense attraction between them. She would have to go "cold turkey."

This would be their last weekend together, the last time they would ever make love. Why not enjoy it? Wasn't Tor her very best friend? She would make the final hours sweet for both of them.

Relaxing in his arms, she more than responded to his kiss; she initiated a campaign of her own, her hands beginning a battle to bring him into submission to her desire. As well as he knew her, she knew him.

"That's right," he whispered. "Don't fight it. Let it happen the way it always does for us." He lifted his head. "We're good together, baby. Don't you forget it!" He made a low growling sound of male satisfaction as his lips foraged along her jaw and over her chin to nibble along her neck.

"I know," she gasped, "but all good things come to an end."

His tongue licked fire into the hollows of her throat. "Don't say that. There's no end for us. Our time together has proven that. I want you more all the time."

But not enough to marry me, she thought on a note of infinite sadness. Not enough to want to plan a future together.

"Oh, Tor," she whispered. "I just want—"

"Don't say any more," he pleaded. "Just let me love you. Let me show you what we have, what you say you want to throw away." His body hardened beneath her, luring her with his masculine desire. His passion for her was real and pressing and very seductive in its force.

His hands ran hit-and-run raids over her slender body, leaving her defenseless. There was no one like him, she admitted. She was afraid there never would be anyone to replace him. But that was silly. Of course there would.

She slipped her hands inside his shirt and performed a series of rapid attack-and-retreat maneuvers, leaving him panting with longing. She refused to satisfy him, but instead slid her lips down the cord of his neck onto his chest. With her tongue she worried the blond pelt that lightly covered him, finding his nipples and wringing a sighing gasp from his throat.

"Do you like this?" she demanded, mimicking his questions. "And this? This?"

With each pause she advanced, bolder and bolder in her movements. She lifted herself from his lap and removed his belt, unfastened his jeans, then tugged until he let her pull them from his sinewy limbs. Slowly, deliberately, she removed her own clothing, then knelt beside him on the braided rug.

His hands cupped her breasts reverently as she leaned toward him. His mouth covered hers in an endless kiss of endless questions. But soon neither of them cared about the answers or the questions, as their passion built to a crescendo, taking them both beyond thought.

For an eternity, she lay against Tor's lean body, held securely in his strong, gentle arms.

Some time later she opened her eyes at his touch on her abdomen. He caressed her in a kneading manner. With his head propped on his hand, he gazed at her tenderly. "Do you really think you could give this up?" he asked.

"I won't have to. I'll share sex with my husband."

His fingers dug into the wall of abdominal muscle, causing her to wince. He lessened the force. "If I thought belting you one would make you see the light, I'd do it."

She lifted a languid fist to him. "Anytime you're ready," she said, accepting the challenge.

He sighed heavily. "All right, explain to me in words of one syllable just what it is you want and why."

Unfolding her fist, Meli stroked the flat plane of his cheek. With one finger, she traced the stubborn line of his chin. Idly she wondered why they hadn't quarreled more often during their association. This was the longest and most serious disagreement they had ever had. Most of their arguments had been philosophical, she being a staunch conservationist, he opting for moderation in conflicts between business and the environment.

"Meli." His tone warned of his impatience.

"Part of what you said about being thirty was correct. I'm not old, but I am coming to the end of my childbearing years. If my husband and I want children, I would like to have them before I'm thirty-five."

Tor's face brightened. "Ah-ha. So that's what this is all about. I should have realized. It's the maternal instinct, a driving force to ensure the survival of the species."

"I don't have any driving force to have a child," she denied.

"All women do, more or less," he said with an air of authority, and Meli rolled her eyes toward heaven. "Then why do you think you want children?" he demanded, seeing her action.

"Well, for one thing, I like the Robinson teenagers. They're fun and nice to be around. I'd like to watch a child grow up like that. For another thing, a friend of mine over at Polebridge has a new baby girl. She's cuddly, of course, but interesting as a person, too. She already shows definite likes and dislikes at five months."

"Did you ever stop and think what our children would look like, yours and mine?" he asked softly.

Her heart missed a painful beat. "No," she said shortly. "I want a father for my children."

He ignored her statement. "Tall and blond with blue eyes. We're a combination that can't miss."

She scoffed at his idea. "I'm not into genetic engineering. All I want are normal, healthy children, not a Nordic basketball team. And only if my husband wants them too. It would have to be a mutual decision." Her views were very firm about this.

"All right, so you're going to have great sex and healthy children from this marriage. What else?"

"Companionship," she answered promptly.

"Huh," he grunted.

"When I was in New York, I found it difficult to go out alone, although I screwed up my courage and did it. I used taxis to get from the hotel to the theaters or concert halls, but I really was afraid of getting mugged. A city that large is just a tad intimidating for a girl from the north woods." She chuckled, remembering her first trip and how she had lived on nerves, forcing herself to get out and do the things she had decided to do while safe at home.

"So a husband would provide free escort service. Typical," he remarked.

"What does that mean?"

"You women are always dragging men off to some boring evening when we'd much rather stay home and watch football."

"Typical male complaint. You'd all get lazy and develop beer bellies if it weren't for women," she said with breezy assurance.

He held up a hand and counted on his fingers. "Sex, kids, and companionship. Anything else?"

There was laughter lurking in the depths of his eyes and around the edges of his lips. He was enjoying himself now, sure that he had everything under control. He wasn't one to admit defeat; she knew that.

Feeling a definite surge of affection for him, she patted his hand, which rested just below her rib cage. "You haven't counted the three Ls."

"What are they?" He waited expectantly for the answer.

"Love, laughter, and loyalty, the three most important ingredients for a successful relationship."

"We have those, Meli," he said quietly. "I care very much for you. I want you to be happy. That's why I'm so concerned about this half-baked idea of yours." His hand turned and their fingers laced together.

She spoke past the lump in her throat. "I know that, darling. And I love you. You're my very best friend—"

"Dammit! I'm your lover!" he exclaimed.

"Yes," she replied evenly. "That's icing on the cake of our friendship as far as I'm concerned." Her brow contracted in an earnest frown. "But Tor, I need more than an occasional piece of cake. A person needs daily bread for sustenance."

He lost his temper entirely. "Bread!" he snarled. "Bread!"

Thrusting his feet into his pants, he dressed quickly, pulling on his shoes without bothering with socks, and slammed out of the house without his jacket.

Meli sat up, shivering in the sudden stir of cold air. "Spoiled brat!" she yelled at the closed door. "I hope you freeze!"

She gathered her clothes and carried them to her bedroom, then took her shower and slipped on her granny gown and a warm fleece robe before padding back down in her quilted booties. The living room was still empty. So let him stay out and sulk. She hoped his toes turned into ice cubes and fell off!

Having chosen a new book, she plunked down on the sofa and began reading, making her eyes stay on the printed page instead of looking up at every little sound.

An hour later, Meli was prowling anxiously from window to window, trying to penetrate the opaque velvet of the night, seeking a glimpse of movement, a shadowy hulk standing among the trees. Nothing. Not a sign of him. She turned on the front porch light in case he needed a guide back to the cabin.

Thirty minutes after that, she sighed in resignation

as she went upstairs to dress in warm clothes. She
had seen bear tracks up on the ridge that morning. If
they had been fresh, she would have said something,
insisted on returning home; but she had judged them
to be at least a day old or older.

The Glacier Park area was one of the last strong-
holds of the grizzly in the States. The bears would
be coming out of hibernation now, hungry and
grouchy. The mothers would have their cubs out of
the den and would be very protective. Woe to anyone
who got between a mama grizzly and her babies!

Not that Meli thought there were any bears lurking around the camp; there hadn't been any there in
years, but still . . .

Pulling on a warm parka, she threw Tor's coat
over her arm, picked up the flashlight and went out
into the dark. First she crossed the road to the
campsites, walking along the creek that murmured
ghostly prophecies in the pale moonlight.

The night was eerily quiet, as if the world existed
in a vacuum. Meli could hear the sound of her own
breath rushing in and out of her lungs; her heart beat
in gigantic leaps within her chest.

The snap of a twig behind her caused every hair to
stand on end. She froze. For a full two minutes, she
watched and waited. Then, feeling ridiculous, she
plodded on, calling Tor's name softly as she went.

She circled the edge of the creek until she reached
the boathouse and dock. She looked for him at the
end of the pier. Failing to find him there, she roamed
up the other stream beside the cabins. Cutting across

the center of the loop next to the lodge, she heard hearty laughter and a distinctive voice loudly proclaiming, "I found it!"

Puffing up with anger, she stomped up the front steps and into the main room. There, seated around a table containing a jigsaw puzzle, was the miscreant wanderer with the three Robinson teenagers.

Greta, pouring cups of hot cocoa, greeted Meli warmly. "There you are! I just tried to call and invite you down for cocoa and fresh cinnamon bread." She grabbed another mug from a shelf and filled it to the brim.

Fletcher stood. "Here, pull up a chair," he invited, then did it for her. He indicated the seat near him in front of the fireplace.

Eighteen-year-old Sam spoke up. "Come over and help us with this puzzle. At the rate we're going, it'll take till Christmas."

Meli walked over and saw that the design was jelly beans, thousands of them. "That *is* a hard one," she admitted, avoiding a direct look at Tor and staying out of his reach.

Troy, a shy seventeen-year-old with a massive crush on her, grinned at her, ducked his head, and got a little red on the neck.

"Gretchen, come help," her mother requested.

Gretchen, two years younger than Troy, reluctantly started to get up. Hero worship was written all over her young face each time she glanced at Tor. It was obvious that she didn't want to give up her place next to him.

"I'll serve," Meli said, tossing her coat and Tor's on a chair and placing the flashlight on the accompanying table.

Seducer of maidens, she thought unfairly, giving Tor one scathing flash from stormy blue eyes before going over to take the tray from Greta.

For the next half hour she sat in front of the fire and made small talk with Fletch and Greta while the other four worked on the puzzle. The scrape of a chair caught her attention, and from the corner of her eye she saw Tor stretch his lean frame, then gather their coats.

"Ready to go, Meli?" he called across the room.

"In a minute," she said coolly, refusing to let him order her around. She finished a discussion with her manager before leisurely rising and taking her cup to the sink and rinsing it.

Tor held her coat for her, then slipped his on. Taking the flashlight with one hand and Meli's elbow with the other, he said good night and escorted her out. Once outside, she pulled her arm from his grasp and rammed her hands into her pockets, stalking along at great speed which he matched easily with his long stride.

At her house, she hung up her coat, turned the porch light out, and went up to change into her nightgown again. This was accomplished in stiff-lipped silence.

With the robe belted tightly around her, she returned to the living room, where Tor sat in the big chair next to the sofa. He had kicked off his shoes and propped his feet on a low hassock. The fire had been built up to a sparkling blaze.

Taking a position in the corner of the couch, she asked, "What time will you be leaving tomorrow?" She kept her face carefully bland, although inside she was burning to hit him or do something equally belligerent.

Tor studied her expression for a long time before answering. His eyes roamed over each feature with a haunting tenderness that almost softened her anger.

"Well?" she demanded.

"Whenever you're ready," he said.

His answer caught her off guard and he smiled at the sudden change in her. "Wha-what do you mean?" she stuttered.

With a graceful movement of his hand, he surrendered. "I'm going to do what you want—take you to Atlanta and find you a husband."

She protested, "I can't get ready in one day!"

He was prepared with a plan. "Then I'll go ahead and set up some dinners and parties for you. You can join me, say, by the end of the month. That's over two weeks from now—"

"You really mean it?" she broke in.

"Yes."

She had a frantic rush of thoughts. Foremost in her mind was the realization that he was willing to help her . . . but further back was a sensation of pain that she wasn't willing to recognize. This was what she wanted, what by careful analysis she had arrived at as the right path for her.

She began planning feverishly. "I'll need a place to stay, nice but not too expensive . . ."

"You can stay at my place. My house is plenty big enough for the two of us."

"Tor, I can't. It wouldn't be fair to my husband."

"For Pete's sake, you don't have one yet!" he thundered at her.

The soft curves of her mouth hardened to granite. "I know that." She bit off the words. "But what man in his right mind is going to want to marry a woman who is living with another man?"

"My stepfather did," he reminded her, and savagely enjoyed the momentary discomfort his words brought.

"But I want a different relationship," she said firmly. "One based on honesty and . . . and loyalty. The kind of marriage my parents had."

His fingers drummed on the smooth vinyl of the chair arm. "What if I provided you with a chaperon? I have a cousin who would stay with us, I think. She's older and perfectly respectable. That should take care of your sense of propriety." His smile was sardonic.

Meli considered the implications of staying in Tor's house. She would be able to stay longer if she lived with him . . . in his house, she corrected. Being far from wealthy, she had calculated to the penny what she could spend on this venture. It wasn't a great deal, especially considering the price of the outfits she had bought in New York earlier in the spring.

But would Tor leave her alone if they were sleeping in the same house? More to the point, would she be able to resist him?

"Tor, you do realize that if I come to Atlanta, I won't . . . we won't . . . that is, we can't . . ."

"Sleep together anymore?" he asked laconically.

"Yes." She sighed with relief that he understood.

"Mm-hmm, I understand that."

Something about the way he said it made her suspicious. "I want your word that you won't try anything if I do stay at your place. Promise that you won't make love to me."

She held his gaze bravely, knowing by the very stillness of his face that there was turbulence within.

"All right," he said heavily. "I give you my word that I'll keep my hands off you for the duration of your visit. And I'll stay out of your bed."

"Then I'd be glad to accept your invitation if your cousin can make it." She smiled brilliantly at him. "Thank you."

She couldn't see his face as he bent over the fire and added another log. "We'll see how it goes," he said gruffly, his back still toward her. "Just how long do you think you'll need to find this dream man and bewitch him into proposing?"

She glared at his broad back. "If that's going to be your attitude, we may as well forget it. You'll scare off any man who might be interested." Another thought struck her. "Do you know any eligible bachelors? Not some clod that nobody would want or some castoff who's impossible to live with. It's all right if he's been divorced once, but not more than that."

Tor glanced over his shoulder at her. The fire highlighted the side of his face and backlighted his hair to fiery gold. He looked like a flaming god.

Meli turned away, unable to bear the sight. Somehow this was more difficult than she had anticipated.

"Picky, aren't you?" he teased. "I remember all your requirements, my love. Maturity, sense of humor, likes kids, terrific in bed, a faithful lover. Say! Why don't we have them fill out a questionnaire? Save a lot of time that way."

His grin was so infectious that she had to laugh. "I hadn't thought of that. But how are we going to know that they're all they say they are?" she quipped.

Tor settled on the sofa beside her, taking her hand and idly caressing it between both of his. "Well, former wives or mistresses could vouch for the lover part. And we could crack a few jokes to check out his sense of humor."

Meli started giggling. "If your jokes are anything like past ones, he'd look pained instead of amused."

He assumed an injured air. "Well, really! I'll ignore that snide remark. Now, we can hire someone to seduce him . . ."

"What for?"

"To see if he's loyal."

"I'll handle that part," she said. "Also the maturity and kids."

He shrugged. "Then that should take care of everything. Are you ready to go to bed?"

At her nod, he pulled her to her feet and sent her up the steps with a pat on her rear. In the bath, she washed her face and brushed her teeth. Then she combed her hair, deciding that she needed a new style. When she got to Georgia, she would have it trimmed and shaped.

Back in her room she pulled off her robe and glanced down at her flannel nightgown. With sudden dislike, she removed it and stuffed it in a drawer. From a tissue-filled box, she lifted out another gown.

This one was midnight blue, made of silk and lace that dipped low between her breasts, hugged the slenderness of her waist, and tumbled to the floor in a shimmering cascade.

Her heart beat fast when she heard Tor's steps on the staircase. She pivoted to face him when he entered.

"Meli!" He was stunned. Swiftly he closed the space between them. "Witch. What are you trying to do to me?" His hands caressed her bare arms.

"What do you mean?"

A harsh look preceded his answer. "You want to break off with me and find a husband, yet you come to me on our last night dressed like this."

She licked dry lips and tried to explain. "You see me in winter clothes so much. I thought something different, something special, would be nice."

"Nice isn't the word." He smiled and pulled her to him, burying his face against the side of her neck. "Babe, you're driving me crazy," he muttered thickly.

"I didn't mean . . ."

"No, it's okay."

He picked her up as easily as if she were a doll,

carried her to the bed and laid her on it. Not taking his eyes off her, he began undressing. "I feel like a miser counting his gold," he said, and a fierceness entered his dark eyes. For a chilling moment, he resembled a golden eagle circling high, intent on finding the unguarded instant for the plunging dive.

Meli shivered under the impact of his study.

"Cold?" he asked softly, settling beside her. His hands swept in long caresses down the silky material along her spine, continuing over her hips and her thighs before making the return trip.

"No," she whispered, lying. She felt as if she had fallen into a snowbank, but she knew she would soon be warm as the fire inside her began to build.

His lips followed the vee of lace to its point and back up to her throat. "You'll have no trouble weaving your spell around your man, beautiful witch of the north," he murmured against her skin as he nibbled the sensitive area behind her ear. "I've been enchanted from the moment we met."

"Oh, Tor," she cried softly. "I don't want to hurt you. I never meant for you to be injured. You're my best—"

His mouth smothered the rest of the sentence. He invaded her with deliberate force, stifling her fervent declaration, driving the words right out of her mind.

Relentlessly he pursued his sensual attack until she was moaning and twisting beneath him. Between them lay the knowledge that this was the last time, the very last. It lent an urgency never before present in their coming together. Again and again he carried them to the brink of the magic flight, but each time he held them back as if he could make the night last forever. Finally even his will was overcome by the intensity of their passion and together they soared beyond knowledge into ecstasy.

When she became aware of his weight, she stirred slightly. He rolled to his back with a weary sigh, as if he had just returned from a long, impossibly hard journey.

At last, they moved. With heavy, languid motions they climbed beneath the covers. Tor turned off the light and laid an arm across the damp silk covering her body.

"I'll keep my word," he promised, "about not seducing you. But I warn you, I'll try everything else in my power to get you to change your mind about this husband hunt."

Chapter Five

The going-away party at the Robinsons' several days later was a hilarious event, with Meli the recipient of much joking advice given by the three young people. Naturally she hadn't told them she was planning on getting married, but they suspected that things were changing between her and her boyfriend since she was going to visit his home. Meli let them think what they wanted. She responded to their jibes good-naturedly and ignored the silent worry in Greta's light blue eyes.

With Fletch, she went over the schedule of activities for the month of May. The summer season started in June and she felt just a tiny bit guilty for taking off during this time of preparation for the tourist rush.

"We're booked solid the last of June and all of July and August. Keeping the store stocked is the hardest thing," she explained. The Robinsons had arrived in September of the previous year and had missed the madhouse of the middle of the season.

"Claude is due in on the fifteenth of June, as soon as he can get away from his teaching duties. He knows what to do."

Claude was a music teacher at a small community college in Ohio. He had been a guest last year and had initiated several evenings of campfire sing-alongs. They had proven so popular that Meli had paid him to stay the remainder of the summer. This year he was going to be a sort of recreational director, arranging wildlife studies and story hours as well as musicals.

"Make sure that the parents and children know that the area on the other creek is off limits to them," she continued. "The avid fishermen don't like the idea of kids poking around their gear while they're out fishing, or bothering them when they're in camp."

Fletch chuckled. "I noticed that a lot of the men rented cabins this time and are bringing their families with them."

Meli nodded. "Several told me they were pleased with the new arrangements. Their wives wouldn't sleep in a tent, much less in a sleeping bag in the open."

"I don't blame them!" Greta shivered convincingly. "Bugs and snakes!"

"Oh, Mom!" scolded a chorus of young voices.

"That wasn't my imagination I saw slithering along the dock last fall."

Toward the end of the party, Greta had the children bring out a chocolate cake. Meli, as the guest of honor, got to cut it into moist wedges over which Greta spooned real whipped cream. For a few minutes, only the sounds of forks against china and the night song of insects broke the silence.

"That was delicious, Greta. With food like this, your kitchen can't fail to be a big hit this summer." Meli wiped her mouth and stood. "I've got to finish packing if I'm going to be ready to leave at the crack of dawn in the morning. Who's going to drive me to the airport?"

"Mom and Dad," Gretchen replied so glumly that they all laughed.

Meli said good night, walked back to her cabin, and resumed her packing. Now that her departure was imminent, she was filled with misgivings. "Which is only normal," she assured herself.

She felt that she had come to the end of a period of her life, and a feeling of loss was to be expected. Also to be expected was uncertainty about the future. After all, acquiring a husband was a major change in a person's life.

She removed her new suit from its hanger. Instead of folding it, she sat on the large bed, her fingers nervously picking at the nubby texture of the soft pink material. She had bought the outfit in New York at Bloomingdale's. Her first designer ensemble. Would it be worth the price she had paid?

Her expression became pensive and her eyes darkened. Somewhere in the years to come, Tor would be only a casual acquaintance, someone she used to know. She probably wouldn't see him at all—maybe a chance meeting at an airport or in a theater lobby, perhaps at a party. They would chat briefly and go on.

For long minutes she sat there, lost in thought, until she realized she was crushing the soft fabric of her suit. She smoothed it out and put it back on the hanger, deciding to carry it in the suitbag she had recently purchased.

Quickly now, she finished and snapped the cases closed, then lined them up in a neat row for the next day's journey. She glanced around the homey room, absorbing its warmth and coziness, noting her travel clothes laid out on a rocking chair.

She got into the bed, turned out the light, and lay still, listening to the wind and the whisper of the trees. Trees are night creatures, becoming most active when people go to bed, she thought, recalling a childhood fancy. Envisioning her own roots reaching deeply into the thin, rocky soil of the mountains, she knew a painful wrench at the thought of leaving.

The next morning, Greta was tearful at the small local airport where Meli would catch a shuttle flight to a major airport.

"Somehow I feel I'm losing a daughter," the older woman said. "You won't come back to us." She mopped wet eyes.

"Of course I will," Meli protested, her own eyes bright with unshed tears.

At last she was buckled into her seat on the small plane, and her journey began. From Kalispell she flew to Denver, changed planes, and arrived in Atlanta in the late afternoon, tired but excited. Tor was waiting for her.

He looked incredibly handsome in a soft suede jacket of honey tan, tweed pants, and a blue shirt. She watched his vivid eyes sweep the crowd, pass her, stop, and dart back as he did a double take. She grinned broadly.

Her summer-weight wool suit was the very latest fashion. The smooth-fitting skirt hugged her hips and had a flirtatious slit over one knee. The puffed sleeves and nipped-in waistline looked good on her tall, slender form. The gray-blue color of the suit contrasted with the white of her blouse and accented the smoky quality of her eyes.

"Hello," she said softly as Tor stopped in front of her, only his eyes speaking.

"My God," he said at last. "You're going to knock 'em dead, honey."

She laughed gaily at his exaggerated drawl. Slipping her hand into the crook of his arm, she suggested they find her luggage and get out. With the first moment of awkwardness past, they talked easily while watching the baggage mosey along the conveyor in the pickup area.

"That's mine," she said, pointing to a large suitcase. "And that one. Here's the small one and the suitbag." She grabbed it while Tor hefted the two large pieces.

"Is this it?" he asked wryly.

"No, there's one more. Here it comes!" Reaching sideways between two people, Meli retrieved the last piece of matched luggage, which she had received as a gift when she went off to college. Until this year, it had rarely been used. But after four trips plus this one, it was showing the little scuffs and scratches of the seasoned traveler's baggage.

"It takes four cases and a suitbag to carry a couple of pairs of jeans?" Tor teased as he stored the items in the trunk of his car.

He was in for a surprise, she thought happily, climbing in the passenger's side of the luxury automobile when he opened the door for her. Maybe he had seen her in only jeans and cords, but from now on he wouldn't.

It had taken long hours of poring over magazines and catalogs, but she had put together a chic, sophisticated wardrobe and she thought he would be proud of her when he introduced her to his friends.

Tor drove north toward his home. "I'll take you on a grand tour later. I figured you'd be tired today."

"Yes, I am."

She glanced at Tor. He seemed different, almost a stranger in his city clothes. Her doubts assailed her again, and she wished she were back home where everything was safe and familiar. But then her lips firmed stubbornly. She wasn't going to back down.

Calm once more, she watched the passing scenery with increasing enjoyment. When they had passed through the downtown area, the city assumed a country look with lots of trees and shrubs in landscaped settings that had a natural look.

"Oak," she said, naming the trees, "poplar, magnolia. Oh, look at that house!" She craned her neck to watch the mansion until it was out of sight. "I feel like I'm in *Gone With the Wind*."

Tor handled the car with casual skill. The streets were winding now and hilly, and the signs said West Paces Ferry, Nancy Creek, Northside Parkway, Paces Mill, Akers Mill Road. Then they seemed to leave the town behind.

As they passed stone walls and elaborate gates, she realized that they were in an area of exclusive estates.

"Wow," she exclaimed sotto voce, seeing a girl racing a beautiful horse across a green meadow. She liked to ride. Maybe there was a stable nearby. As she turned to ask, Tor swung the wheel, turning into a drive flanked by two massive limestone towers. Fieldstones arched away on either side, forming a waist-high wall that enclosed a park of rolling lawns and tall trees.

"Where are we?" she asked, avidly interested in her surroundings.

"Home," he said on a note of satisfaction. "That stream is a small branch running into Sope Creek, which runs into the Chattahoochee River. The country club is thataway." He indicated the direction with his thumb pointing over his shoulder.

Meli fell totally silent as they proceeded up the winding drive. He stopped in front of a dazzling white mansion that had a two-story middle part and two wings sweeping forward from each side, forming almost a semicircle around the edge of the limestone block courtyard. She gulped as she stepped out of the car and stood on suddenly shaky legs.

A man came out of the house. Tor introduced him as James, the bailiff of the place, and advised her to stay on the man's good side. The two men smiled with the easy familiarity of long association. Tor tossed the car keys to James, who went to the trunk to get her cases.

Meli remained stiffly in place until Tor took her arm and guided her up a broad, shallow flight of steps into a marble-paved entrance hall. She slowly surveyed the two-story-tall room. White marble with green tracings. Silk-covered walls, palest green. The polished patina of satinwood inlaid on teak.

Her entire cabin would nearly have fitted into the space she was now staring at.

"Oh, Tor," she whispered, her voice tight with hurt accusation. "Why didn't you tell me?"

She had known he had money, but it had never occurred to her that he lived this far above her own expectations. Because she was her own boss, so to speak, she had assumed they were on an equal social level. Now she saw how far from the truth that assumption had been. It was like stepping on a land mine. All her plans were blown to smithereens. Instinctively, she moved closer to him.

"Don't you like it?" His voice had a curious

quality to it. He circled her narrow waist with strong arms, recognizing but puzzled by her need for reassurance from him.

"Like it? It's beautiful. That isn't the point." She spread her fingers over his chest and stared at them, unable to lift her eyes to his as she felt the aching smart of tears in them. Her grand ideas really did seem harebrained now.

"What is, then?" he asked.

Meli finally raised her troubled gaze to his. She answered him as honestly as she knew how. "I have no intention of marrying a tenth-grade dropout; by the same token, do you really think any of your friends would be interested in marrying a woman from the north woods who owns a fishing camp?" Tears clogged her throat. "My house would fit in your hallway," she finished huskily.

His arms tightened, drawing her to his chest. "Have I ever made you feel that your home was less than mine?"

She shook her head. Pressing her forehead to his shirtfront, she accepted the comfort of his arms without question. His cheek touched her temple.

"You're a witty, intelligent, capable woman, the equal of anyone I know," he went on persuasively. "And a beautiful broad that any man would give his eyeteeth to be seen with."

She laughed a little at his teasing note.

He squeezed her. "Meli, look at me," he requested in a rough whisper.

She raised her solemn face to his. Staring into his

eyes, she saw the message he was sending to her. His look told her that she was desirable, lovely in many ways. Her lips trembled into a smile.

"Meli," he said hoarsely. "Meli, I . . ."

The door opened behind them and James came in carrying two of her suitcases. Walking around them, he continued through an archway into the guest wing to the left of the foyer. Tor released her and indicated that they should follow.

James led the way into an elegant bedroom furnished with antique furniture and gilt-framed oil paintings. The four-poster bed was covered by an elaborate lace counterpane. The wallpaper design was a misty floral spray that looked like a watercolor drawing.

Two doors, fourteen feet high and reaching almost to the ceiling, opened onto a view of rolling back lawn. A mass of pink-flowered shrubs erupted into color against a backdrop of verdant woods. It was unbelievably lovely.

"Leave the doors open," Tor told James, who had moved to close them. The man smiled at Meli and went to get the rest of her bags.

"This is heavenly," she declared, with a sweep of her arm that took in the room and the outside view at the same time. "Thank you, Tor. Has your cousin arrived?"

He busied himself opening her luggage for her. "Yes," he said. "Paula arrived this morning. She's anxious to meet you, so we'll go out to the veranda when you're ready. I thought we'd unpack anything that needs to be hung up right away. Do you want a maid to do it for you?"

"I'll do it," she said quickly.

"I thought you'd want to. Tell James when you need something. He runs the place like clockwork, so I've never had a housekeeper."

Tor unbuckled the strap on the suitbag and unzipped it. He took out the pink suit, nodded appreciatively, then hung it up for her in a large closet. He lifted out the long, black taffeta skirt that was the basis of her formal wear. "What's this?"

"It's my long skirt. To wear to concerts and things," she explained when he looked askance at it.

"This won't do, sweetheart. You'll look like somebody's maiden aunt. Don't you have any other evening dresses?"

Meli had chosen her skirt with great care and after lengthy consultation with the manager of the formal clothing department at a large department store. She knew it was correct.

"Let me show you how it works." She took out a white lace overskirt and held it up to the taffeta along with a frothy lace blouse that was very feminine. "See? Now here's a different look." She held up a gold lamé top and a black patent belt, then a midnight blue silk chemise blouse.

Tor cocked one dark brow when she finished. "Charming," he said sincerely. "But, honey, you can't wear the same skirt to everything."

She grinned. "I'll have to. It's all I have. How many formal affairs will we be attending this month?" she asked, thinking the answer would be two or three. She took the black skirt from him and placed it in the spacious closet with her other things.

"Tomorrow night there's a dance in your honor at the country club . . ."

"My honor!" She was aghast.

"Sure." His grin was mischievous. "How else did you think I was going to launch you into society?"

"You're giving it?"

"I'm sponsoring you, yes." He nodded complacently. "We're having guests for dinner on Saturday night. Sunday afternoon is an art exhibit and tea party at the gallery. Monday night we're going to the mayor's reception, and Tuesday we have a dinner with friends of mine—he's president of a local bank. Then on Friday it's the symphony, and Saturday is the Masque of the Spring Moon Ball. You'll need something really scrumptious for that. All the women dress to kill and are insulted if they aren't written up in the paper."

Meli's knees went more than weak; they gave out entirely at this listing of events. She sat down shakily on the nearest needlepoint chair. "Oh, Tor, what have you done? What have *I* done?" she moaned, feeling like Pandora.

He sank to his haunches in front of her as James returned with the rest of her things. Ignoring the presence of a third party, Tor clasped her hands, his thumbs rubbing soothingly over her skin. "I'm doing exactly what you wanted. Don't worry, there'll be plenty of husband material around." He swiveled around. "Don't you think we'll be able to find her a husband, James?"

James looked about fifty. He had lots of gray in his hair and bags under his brown eyes. He was of average height, slender with an erect carriage. He studied Meli seriously and she waited anxiously for his verdict. "I shouldn't think it would be any trouble at all," was his pronouncement.

She was inordinately relieved, for some reason trusting the older man's judgment. Tor gave her a see-I-told-you-so grin. He stood when James departed, telling her to meet him in the foyer in ten minutes and they would have a drink on the terrace before dinner with Paula. "Take your jacket off if you want, but don't change," he advised, going out the door and closing it behind him.

Sighing wearily, Meli went over to the open doors and looked at the darkening garden. Her mind restlessly replayed the events that had happened since her arrival at Tor's spectacular home. Why had she not realized the opulence in which he lived? Because in Montana, Tor acted just like everyone else—no airs, no rich-boy attitudes.

He had washed dishes, mopped floors, mended roofs, weighed and cut bait, served behind the counter of her small store. Not once had he made her or the Robinsons or anyone feel socially inferior.

She pressed the back of one hand against her hot forehead. "Oh, lordy," she groaned, thinking of the things she had asked him to do. Once he had unstopped the commode for her. That memory brought forth a tiny giggle.

Misty-eyed, she stared out at the cloud of pink flowers.

He had been very nice to her in the hall a few minutes ago, correctly interpreting and calming her fears. What had he been about to say in that heart-stopping moment before James returned? He had been so intense.

Sighing deeply, she knew she was slowly regaining her usual control. This next month wasn't going to be easy, but she was going to get through it. Maybe she would find a husband.

In the bathroom, which had pink marble, gold fixtures, she splashed water on her face and hands, then found her makeup kit and redid her face. Hurriedly, she ran a comb through her hair, then dashed down the hall to meet Tor.

He was standing in front of a lighted curio cabinet. She stopped beside him and gazed at the figurines and items locked inside. Many glittered with gold and fine gems; any one of them had probably cost more than the furnishings of her entire house. She grinned wryly.

"Come on." Tor led her along a corridor and out a door to a wide gallery overlooking the back lawn. The gallery had probably once been a porch but was now glassed in.

A woman, blond and in her late thirties, was seated in a fanback wicker chair when they entered. She stood and came forward, a welcoming smile lighting her face. "Meli," she said in greeting.

"This is my cousin, Paula," Tor said. "Your chaperon."

He and Paula laughed while Meli looked indignant at his teasing. The women shook hands.

"I really do appreciate your coming here," Meli said. "Do you live in Atlanta?"

"No, I have a little place further upstate," Paula answered. "It's nice for me to get to come to town and do the social whirl once in a while."

Tor ushered them into chairs and James came in with a tray of drinks for them. Meli found that the stemmed glasses contained a mixture of dry wine and soda, chilled to perfection. It was tart and refreshing.

"Paula is an artist," Tor explained after James left.

Meli was fascinated. "Oh, what do you like to do best?"

"Landscapes," Paula replied. "But I tend to isolate myself in my groves of peach and pecan trees, so sometimes I accept a commission to do a portrait. I'd like very much to do yours if you'd let me. I can show you some of my work."

"Mine?" Meli was flattered to think someone would want to paint her.

"You'll make a radiant bride. I'd like to capture that." The artist smiled engagingly.

An embarrassed frown creased the younger woman's face. "Do you know . . ."

"That you're here to find a husband? Yes."

Meli turned on Tor. "Does everyone know?" she demanded. "Do you plan to auction me off at that dance tomorrow night?"

He threw back his head and laughed, hugely

amused by her outburst. At last he reassured her.
"Only James and Paula know of your plans. The
dance is just the regular Friday night bash. I was
kidding you earlier. I thought we would go, but we
don't have to if you'd rather not."

Paula interrupted before Meli could think of
something scathing to say to him. "Tor said you were
worried about getting old, but you look rather young
to me."

Distracted, Meli explained her reasons. "I'm
twenty-nine, and if I'm to have children, I'd like it to
be before I'm thirty-five."

Paula laughed gently. "Honey, you have nothing
to worry about. I'm forty-nine. At my age, you
should worry maybe, but not at yours."

"I thought you were in your late thirties!" Meli
peered at her hostess. "You don't have a wrinkle."

"Oh, you should have seen the grandmother that
Tor and I have in common. At sixty, she looked like
a girl. But to tell you the truth, I try to remember
not to squint when I paint."

Meli nodded in understanding. "Look." She
pointed to her smooth brow. "I already have a little
frown line."

Tor made a little snort, which the women ignored.

"I want someone to grow old with," Meli continued, telling Paula of her deepest reasons for her
present quest. "Someone who will have known me
before I was wrinkled and sagging, and who, when
he looks at me thirty years from now, will remember
what I looked like when I was smooth and taut."

Paula's blue eyes, so similar to Tor's, went a shade dreamy. "Yes," she agreed. "The eyes of love are so much kinder than others are."

"Right!" Meli relaxed into the cushions of the wicker rocking chair. She knew she was going to like Paula very much. Glancing at Paula's bare fingers, she wondered if the woman had ever been married. Certainly she had once been in love. That was evident in her comprehension of Meli's motives.

From there, the conversation veered to the family tree and Meli learned much about Tor's ancestry from his talkative first cousin. Over an excellent dinner of individual game birds stuffed with a wild rice mixture, they discussed world events, then local happenings.

The women found a wealth of mutual interests. Meli spoke at length about her visits to New York and the exhibitions she had gone to. Paula knew every one of the artists whose work had been on display. They talked about the plays appearing on Broadway and off-Broadway and off-off-Broadway, laughing gaily about an experimental theater they had both been to. Tor joined in, but mostly he seemed content to listen, his cobalt gaze swinging from one woman to the other as their voices rose in animated friendliness.

When they finished the meal, they had coffee in the study, seated in chairs of supple leather around a low, round table. The conversation didn't lag once as the new friends continued to explore each other's minds and experiences. They each told about their homes and the attractions to be found there.

"You would love the high meadows in spring," Meli said.

"The pecan trees are really lovely. Tall and stately with rising limbs that spread like this." Paula demonstrated. "I've painted them a thousand times in every light."

"I'd love to see them," Meli enthused.

"Yes, you must come. Now is a good time. I only live in a farmhouse, though. Don't expect a mansion," Paula warned.

Meli giggled. "You have to come up and visit with me. I have a log cabin—"

With a slight frown, Tor broke into the chatter. "It's nearly midnight. Meli must be tired. I've arranged for James to bring you two to town tomorrow for lunch with me. Then we have some shopping to do for evening dresses. I'll bring you home when we're through."

He rose, took Meli's arm as if she were a child, and led her from the room, hardly letting her say good night to his lovely cousin. She stifled a surge of resentment at his peremptory ways.

At her door he stopped, not releasing his hold on her. His hands moved to her shoulders, bringing her around to face him. His lips dipped toward her. So conditioned was she to welcoming his caresses that she almost forgot the new rules. At the last moment she turned her head.

His kiss landed on her cheek. "What's wrong?" he demanded.

"Nothing. We're not supposed to do this, remember? It's over with us. You can't go around kissing me whenever you feel like it anymore. It wouldn't be fair—"

"To your husband," he finished for her, his brows drawn together in a tight expression.

"Yes," she said, standing her ground.

For a moment she thought he was going to argue with her, but with a smile of good grace, he let her go and stepped back. "I'll try to remember in the future. You might have to remind me once in a while."

"I will," she promised solemnly. She stepped inside her room and closed the door on his somewhat enigmatic smile.

Well, it had been a lovely evening and she was at peace with the world, she thought as she prepared for bed. She quickly washed up and slipped into the silky nightgown she had worn first for Tor. No more flannel for her, at least not on this visit. She was going all out *sexy* from now on.

She turned out the light and climbed into the bed, whose covers had been turned back by some mysterious person. It reminded her of the hotel in New York. She never saw anyone in her room, but clean towels appeared as if by magic, the room was straightened every morning, and every night her gown was placed on the turned-down bed. It had been a little unnerving at first.

Tor had been right about her needing more evening clothes. She had been naive about that, not realizing they would go out so often. She figured she could afford two outfits without terribly straining her budget, but that would be it. She still wanted to get her hair shaped, too. And some new makeup.

She yawned as fatigue overtook her. For a second just before she went to sleep, it seemed that she could feel the familiar pressure of male lips on hers.

Chapter Six

I think we're ready to go," Paula told James. She and Meli followed him out to the car; he held the door for them, then got in himself to act as their driver.

Over breakfast, Paula had explained that the household was comprised of a full-time cook and two maids who shared a cottage and kept the house spotless. A gardening service took care of the grounds. James supervised all of them, handled the household accounts, and looked after Tor "like a mother hen." The man was remarkable.

Paula directed him to the building on Peachtree Street where she and Meli wanted to go. Somehow she had managed to get both of them appointments with her favorite stylist for haircuts and sets.

Meli admired the scenery again and chatted to her

hostess as they rode along. The two women had consulted on clothes over a leisurely breakfast and were dressed in complementary colors, Paula in a green suit with a blue and green print blouse, Meli in her pink suit with a champagne-colored top.

Downtown, amid the tall buildings, Meli was reminded of the phrase "concrete canyons."

"This way," Paula said briskly and started off.

They went into a shop whose reception area looked like someone's home. Meli admired the elaborate decor done with lots of gilt-framed mirrors and brocaded period reproductions of chairs and sofas. The receptionist invited them to be seated and offered them tea, coffee, or cocoa. With the tea they had requested, she brought a small plate of almond cookies and petit fours.

It wasn't until Meli was taken to the back room that she felt as though she were in a beauty shop. There were the driers and sinks lined up in neat rows, and stylists working on their clients. She was given a pink robe to put on.

Paula introduced Meli to Gwen, Paula's own hairdresser, and the two women consulted over a proper cut for Meli. Seated in the chair between them, Meli listened for a bit, then added her opinion.

"Something simple," she said firmly. "I don't roll my hair, so I need a style that can be combed into place."

"We need to open up your face," Gwen said, using her fingers to comb through and hold the hair away from the sides of Meli's face.

"Yes." Paula agreed completely.

After she had sectioned Meli's hair, the stylist began cutting in expert snips. When she used the blow-dryer, she instructed Meli on ways to comb the newly layered hair into many styles. "Here, you do it," Gwen said, and showed her how.

While Paula was getting the same careful analysis and treatment, Meli admired her new appearance. She looked chic, sophisticated.

Gwen had trimmed the top of her hair, leaving it pretty much the same, but she had been ruthless on the sides, cutting and shaping until the hair could be feathered back from Meli's temples, covering only the top half of her ears. In the back, the style was layered until it reached the tops of her shoulders. There, Gwen had allowed the ends to turn under in their natural curl. Meli turned her head from side to side, looking at the back with the aid of a hand-held mirror. The light and dark golden shades blended beautifully. She was very pleased.

"You should have your ears pierced," Gwen advised, glancing up from her work. "Both of you. You have nice ears and should show them off."

At one o'clock, Meli and Paula dashed into Peachtree Plaza where they were supposed to meet Tor for lunch.

"Do your ears hurt?" Paula asked.

Meli shook her head. "Not exactly hurt, but I've never been aware of my earlobes before and I am now," she replied.

"Me, too."

Blue eyes met blue, and they burst into laughter, drawing smiles from the people hurrying around them.

"You two seem to have had an amusing morning," a male voice drawled near them. Tor whistled silently as they turned to face him, a wolfish grin of appreciation appearing on his lean face.

He studied one then the other. The smile left his mouth suddenly and he looked forbidding.

"What is it?" Paula demanded. "Don't you like our new looks?"

His answer seemed terribly important to Meli and she waited anxiously for his opinion. "Very much," he said, escorting them up a series of escalators, then into an elevator with windows all around. A recorded voice welcomed them and pointed out some of the sights, such as Stone Mountain, that could be seen as they rose above the surrounding buildings.

The dining room of the circular skyscraper revolved so that the diners had a changing view of the countryside as they ate.

"What have you done to your ears?" he asked after they were seated. "The lobes are bright pink."

"We stopped at the jeweler's on the way over and had them pierced. I've been meaning to do that for years and couldn't get my courage up. When Meli said she would if I would, well, that decided me." Paula looked back at her menu for a second, then said in a casual aside to Meli, "One needs pierced ears in order to wear valuable stones, don't you think?"

"I suppose." Meli resisted an urge to touch the gold balls of her new earrings.

Tor gave her a glance from under his brows. "Your husband will probably give you diamonds to go with your engagement ring . . . if you perform well on your wedding night," he added close to her ear so Paula couldn't hear. "And I'm sure you will."

Meli experienced a jolt at his words, and flames of embarrassment ran up her cheeks. Her look made it very plain that she resented his jibe.

"Shall I order for you?" he continued easily, apparently not at all daunted by her displeasure.

Nodding, Meli closed the menu and gazed out the window at the countryside, which was verdant with the new green of springtime. There was a haze in the air, but it didn't interfere with her enjoyment.

During the meal, the discussion ranged from the Civil War to civil rights in general. Meli discovered a new facet to Tor as he explained his theories on getting minorities started on the "upwardly mobile" path that most Americans take for granted. He also had a program for recruiting women and training them for higher management positions that she thoroughly approved of.

"I think your corporation would be great to work for," she told him. "Maybe I'll apply for a job."

Tor shook his head. "You're too bossy. There's only one chief and that's me!"

Their lunch consisted of a fish casserole with a creamy sauce and slivers of almonds in it. Steamed vegetables were served with the main course; a salad preceded it and a dessert of custard with fruit followed. Replete, Meli was content to sip her g.ass of white wine and watch the scenery glide by while Tor and his cousin had coffee.

After lunch, Paula wanted to stop in an art gallery to visit with a friend. Tor arranged to pick her up when he and Meli finished shopping. He then took Meli to a shop that she knew at once would be appallingly expensive.

She didn't say anything as they were ushered in and seated on silk-covered chairs. It wasn't until the smiling manager had left them that she whispered urgently to Tor, "I can't afford this place. The prices of these clothes are way beyond my means. These are designer originals."

He smiled and she had the intuition that he had bought clothes here before. Their visit had obviously been prearranged, because a model came out almost at once wearing a lovely evening dress. The manager explained it in detail.

Meli sat as immobile as Stone Mountain while several gowns were paraded out. Inside, she was seething. When they were alone again for a moment, she said angrily, "I want to go!"

"We haven't seen the rest of the collection yet. Don't worry about the expense. I can afford it." He was cool in the face of her anger.

She started to rise, but a hand on her arm restrained her; then the show started again so that she was trapped by her unwillingness to create a scene.

"That one," Tor said. The manager made a note. A few minutes later Tor indicated another dress he liked. Again the choice was noted.

Tor's choices, Meli fumed, with not even a glance in her direction to see what she thought. She may as well have been on the other side of the moon!

He didn't see any other evening outfits he liked. "Now some afternoon dresses. Something dressy enough for an afternoon tea that's also appropriate for a dinner," he explained briefly.

After the manager excused himself, Meli turned on her imperturbable escort. With an effort, she reined in her temper and spoke calmly. "I can't let you buy these clothes for me."

"It's my anniversary gift to you," he said, a caress in his voice.

"I don't want it. It's too much, an insult," she stated flatly.

For a moment he looked dangerous in his silent, forbidding way. Then he said, "Didn't you buy me a warm parka and that padded vest? Did I object?"

"That was different. They were Christmas and birthday gifts. And they didn't cost an arm and a leg, either."

Tor took her gesturing hand between his, holding it trapped. "Those gifts were expensive for you, given the amount of money you had, Meli." His voice deepened as though he were making love to her. "But I could buy you ten dresses and not miss the cash. It's all relative. Don't you see?"

"Yes, I see clearly," she said. "But you're the one who needs enlightenment."

He rolled his eyes upward. "Which I am no doubt about to get."

"Can't you see that if I let you buy me these dresses and introduce me to your rich friends, they'll think I'm one of them?"

"So what, for heaven's sake?"

"So that will be a misrepresentation. They'll think I have all kinds of money to throw around, and I don't. It would be misleading and unfair to my future husband."

He gritted his teeth audibly. "I am rapidly getting sick of that phrase!"

They glared into each other's eyes for what seemed an eternity. Meli felt herself becoming lost in his compelling gaze. In an abrupt shift, he softened.

"Please, darling," he whispered. "I want to do this for you. I want to give you something special to remember our perfect years together. Can't you accept that gracefully? I want very much to give you all that your heart desires. After all, I am your best friend, aren't I?"

"Tor, I don't think this is right—"

"Aren't I?" His hands pressed hers gently.

Sighing, she admitted that he was. For another second he looked at her, and it was like yesterday in the foyer. She wanted to question the message that was revealed in those cobalt depths but the next collection of dresses was ready to be shown.

"Tell me if you see anything you like," he invited.

"Thanks," she said wryly.

He chose a medium blue silk dress that had a

matching bolero with sequins all around the edges and at the cuffs. It could easily go from afternoon to evening. She liked an outfit with a perky pleated white skirt and a floral overblouse with loose, flowing sleeves.

"That's it," Tor said a few minutes later. "She's about the same size as your model, so we'd like to take the first evening gown with us; the other things you can deliver." He turned to Meli, giving orders like a general. "Run and try them on. Hurry. We have other things to get."

Her measurements were taken by a black-clad woman with her hair in a bun. Then the same person helped her to try on the first evening dress that Tor had liked. It had a white underdress which fit her figure perfectly. The seamstress held the sheer overdress for Meli to slip into. It, too, was white but was covered with a garden of brilliantly colored blossoms that started from a hemline border print and rose in graceful sprays to her waist. The six-inch cuffs of the puffed sleeves repeated the motif. Meli was enchanted with it.

She was smiling happily when she joined Tor in the antechamber again, but her smile didn't last long. He insisted on buying a complete line of accessories to go with the outfits: shoes, purses, gloves, and hats.

"I never wear a hat, except for cold weather," she said truthfully.

"I'm sure they wear hats to these functions," he said equably.

"Which functions?" she demanded belligerently.

"Tea parties, art shows."

By the time they picked Paula up in the late afternoon, Meli was hardly speaking to Tor. She was tired and her feet hurt from wearing heels all day. Her earlobes ached, and she found herself fidgeting with the gold balls several times.

Paula spoke from the back seat, where she insisted on riding despite Meli's objections. "Did the war start recently, or has it been going on all afternoon?" She was amused.

Tor had the gall to chuckle.

Meli was desperately near to weeping. This wasn't going to work out at all. She shouldn't have come here. What was she doing parading around in silks like a peacock anyway? Wool was the practical choice for her.

At Tor's suggestion, she went to her room for a nap when they arrived home. She had barely stripped to her underclothes and slipped into a robe when a knock sounded on her door. Tor came in without waiting for her invitation to enter.

"What do you want?" she asked grouchily, slumping onto the bed.

His quick grin was reassuring. "I brought you some ice packs for your ears." He held up two small packs of crushed ice in plastic sandwich bags secured with rubber bands. Wrapping them in washcloths from her bath, he presented them with a little flourish.

"Thank you. That was very thoughtful." She regretted her irritation with him.

"Lie down. Here, I'll arrange your pillows to hold

the packs for you." He helped her get settled on the bed, then sat down beside her, his gaze running over her robe-clad figure with a look that stirred her blood.

Her eyes narrowed suspiciously. Smiling sweetly, she inquired, "How are Paula's ears?"

It took a minute for the words to penetrate. The blood ran under his cheeks in a slight flush of guilt. "Well, uh, fine," he said.

"Did she appreciate the ice packs?"

Tor glared his disapproval of the question. "I haven't taken any to her . . . yet."

"Then I suggest you do so at once. Her ears are just as pink as mine." The innocent smile left her face. "And don't come into my bedroom again, not for any reason!"

He got up from her bed quickly. Standing beside it, he placed his hands on his hips and leaned forward with an injured air. "I simply thought you might be in need of some comforting . . . since I *am* your best friend. For some reason, today seemed to be difficult for you."

His tone was that of a patient adult addressing a child. With a quick movement, he retrieved two pills from his pocket. "I brought you some aspirin," he added, going into the bathroom to get a glass of water.

Meli accepted the pills and drank from the glass he held. After she lay back on the pillows and positioned the plastic bags, she touched him lightly on the sleeve. "Thank you, love," she said.

Waiting until he returned the glass to the bath and

went to the door, she added, "Next time, send James or the maid, please. I wouldn't want any talk to get out about your being in here, especially to my future husband."

He cast her a glance carved in granite and she countered it with the chiseled perfection of her smile. After he went, giving the door a decisive slam, she grinned to herself.

Her former lover was determined to use every device he could think of to persuade her to change her mind. He would keep his word about not seducing her, but he wasn't above compromising her a bit, which would discourage the kind of man she wanted to attract, and attract the type she definitely wanted to discourage. Well, my possessive eagle, your tactics won't work. I see through you as if you were crystal. She drifted off to sleep full of her own purposefulness.

It was dark when the maid woke her. "Miss? Miss? It's time to dress."

"What?" Meli raised herself on one elbow and looked at the clock. It was late. "I didn't mean to sleep so long," she muttered.

The maid lifted the bags of liquid from the bed with a curious glance. Laying them aside, she placed a bed tray across Meli's knees. "I have your supper," the older woman said. She served the meal and then disposed of the ice packs. "I'll be back to draw your bath and help you dress when you're ready. Ring the bell." She pointed to the telephone before departing.

Meli had already examined the instrument and knew of the intercom system that connected the bedrooms, the library, and the kitchen area. You only had to press the intercom button and dial the appropriate number listed beside the phone. The master bedroom number was twenty-one. Were there that many phones in the house?

After a bath, which she managed by herself, Meli stood in the closet trying to decide which outfit to wear. She was not going to be ordered about by Tor on the subject of her clothes. She had attended several dances with her social-climbing husband during his first year of law practice in Butte, so she wasn't a stranger to the social scene.

She took the black skirt and white lace top. As she untied her robe, she heard a soft knock on the door. If that was Tor again . . .

"Who is it?"

The maid answered, and entered when Meli invited her to. The woman was middle-aged and wore a wedding ring. She performed her work with efficiency and a polite formality. Her name was Mrs. Reynolds.

"Mr. Halliday suggested that you wear the dress you purchased today," Mrs. Reynolds said diplomatically when she saw the other clothing on the bed.

"This outfit will do," Meli stated.

She slipped into a fitted chemise of beige and a long slip that matched. The lace blouse went over her head. Mrs. Reynolds zipped the short back zipper. A lace petticoat went on next, then the black skirt. Catching up one side, Meli found the hidden loop at the hem and fastened it on a concealed button at her waist, creating a fluttering cascade of ruffles down her left side and exposing the lace underskirt in a provocative vee.

She wore a gold chain around her throat and another on her wrist. They went nicely with the gold earrings. She was pleased to see that her earlobes appeared normal.

The vee of the tightly fitting lace top echoed the inverted one of her skirt. The beige underclothes gave the arresting impression that perhaps she wore very little underneath the lace. This enticing suggestion was as alluring as the lace was virginal.

Meli applied the makeup she had bought at the beauty shop with a heavier hand than usual. Combining eye shadows of dark blue and misty gray gave her eyes depth to go with the sparkle that was beginning to appear. She dusted her face with a frosty bronze powder that gave her a dewy glow, then highlighted her cheeks by rubbing a little more of the powder along her cheekbones. When she finished, the total picture was one of sophisticated innocence.

Mrs. Reynolds, who had been straightening the bath, hung up Meli's robe and turned back the bed, laying her nightgown neatly across the pillow. Then she looked the younger woman over with a slight smile of approval as Meli slipped into black satin evening sandals and picked up her tiny purse, which was black satin with an ornate floral design embroidered in silk threads the colors of the rainbow. "Good night," she said, holding the door.

Meli replied and hurried out, walking briskly as she went to the library to meet Tor and Paula. She was eagerly anticipating Tor's reaction, but only Paula was present when she entered the room.

"My dear!" Paula exclaimed. "You look ravishing. I'm glad I decided not to go. You'll overshadow everyone there."

Tor's cousin was dressed in lounging pajamas, a book in her hand as she relaxed on the sofa.

Meli found Paula's statement daunting. She realized that she had been counting on the other woman's support during the coming evening. "You're not going?" she said stupidly.

"I have a headache. Tor was kind enough to bring me aspirin . . . and ice packs for my ears." Paula gave Meli a mischievous grin as she said this, and Meli knew that he had confided their conversation to his cousin. Her lips tightened.

"Stand over there by that chair," Paula suddenly requested. She put her book aside and stood, came over to Meli, and arranged her beside a high-backed chair with one hand lying on the winged back and the other holding a single spray of pink flowers taken from a vase on the hearth.

With a nod of satisfaction, Paula grabbed a pencil and pad of paper from the desk and began sketching. Meli started laughing.

"Don't move," Paula pleaded as she drew rapidly on the paper, glancing at Meli from time to time. "I've been itching to do you from the moment we met. You have an indescribable aura of . . ." Her brow wrinkled as she tried to find the word.

A deep voice supplied the answer. "Passionate innocence." Tor strolled in, adjusting the French cuffs of his shirt, which complemented his dark evening suit.

Meli thought he looked more handsome each time she saw him. Pictures of him in his casual honey-tan sports suit, his business suit of the day, and now this formal attire leaped into her mind, contrasting with the memories of him in jeans and plaid shirts.

Whatever he wore, nothing could disguise the lithe movements of his strong, well-trained body, she noted as he came toward her and stood without saying more, letting his expressive eyes tell her of his pleasure in seeing her.

"Stand aside, Tor," Paula barked. "Yes, she does have both passion and innocence," the artist agreed as Tor moved to a chair and waited for her to finish.

Meli was aware of Tor's eyes on her, the look deeply conscious of her as a woman, reawakening her to that fact. Would she ever respond to another man as she did to this one? No, something in her replied with finality.

Paula was speaking softly, almost to herself. "That's it. That's what I want to capture. Don't move, Meli." To Tor she said, "Do you see it? That wariness of experience and the childlike expectation, as if she still believed in Santa Claus."

Meli jerked slightly at the words, while a scowl settled on Tor's features. Her Santa Claus lover, she thought. Not her lover anymore, though. That was all in the past.

He glanced at his watch. "We have to go."

Paula acquiesced, turning the sketch and holding it so Meli and he could see it.

"Nice," Tor said dryly while Meli exclaimed in awed tones. "Come on, we're late as it is."

With a hand on her arm, he led her from the room. James waited in the hall with a fur stole, which he held for Meli. She looked at Tor suspiciously, a stubborn tilt to her chin.

"It was my mother's. You'll need a wrap," he said succinctly.

Dropping her war stance, she let the butler place it around her shoulders. She luxuriated in the thick mink pelt that brushed her neck as she drew it close. "It's lovely. Thank you for letting me wear it."

Tor put her in the front seat of his Mercedes and climbed in the driver's side.

"How far is the country club?" she asked after he turned onto the main road from his drive.

"About five miles." He concentrated on the road, then flicked her a laughing glance. "You look lovely. And I won't get angry if you say I told you so."

"Then you like my outfit?"

"Very much. Charming," he added with a ghost of a laugh. This time the word was more than sincere.

She marveled at the wealth of meaning he could convey with one word. His voice, with its rich undertones, made ordinary statements speak volumes. With a sigh, she settled back to enjoy the ride . . . and calm her nerves.

They passed the meadow where she had seen the horse and rider the day before. Maybe she would meet the girl tonight and they could talk about horses. Maybe she would be invited over to ride. A minute later, they passed wrought-iron gates marking the entrance to that estate.

"I assume you know the people who live next door?" she asked. "I saw a girl on a beautiful horse in one of the fields yesterday."

His answer was unexpectedly short. "Yes, I know them."

Meli decided not to say anything else. Since the rest of the ride was brief, there was no need. When Tor stopped in front of a brilliantly lit building, she hesitated about getting out. After giving the car keys to the valet, he came around to her side, helped her out, and turned her toward the door.

"I'm nervous," she confessed.

His grin was wry. *"You're* nervous! I feel like a father launching his only daughter into society. Let's put our best foot forward," he joked, and urged her inside.

Chapter Seven

M eli examined the pink flowers which bordered the lawn, then strolled across damp grass and through trees to a little stream. The rosy glow of azaleas and the new green of trees, coupled with the mother-of-pearl hues of sunrise, gave the world a radiant warmth that was strange to her. She was used to the brisk coolness of her mountains in the early morning.

Behind her, the sleeping house rose white and gleaming like an enchanted castle. Apparently the occupants didn't start the day early on weekends. She hadn't found anyone about when she explored the kitchen at seven.

Barefoot, she waded into the creek and was delighted to find it as warm as the morning air, nothing like the glacier-fed streams of Montana. "Ouch," she muttered, discovering it also had sharp rocks compared to the rounded ones of her home.

Climbing up the opposite bank, she emerged from the trees and stood beside a wire fence. In the field, like a living memory, was the girl on her horse.

The rider's dark hair, similar in color and glossy shine to the mink Meli had worn last night, was caught in two bunches, one below each ear. As she rode close to the barrier, Meli noted the girl's fawn jodhpurs, and the white silky shirt whose material was so fine she could easily discern the lace bra underneath.

"Good morning," Meli said when horse and rider stopped three or four feet on the other side of the fence and looked at her. Her smile disappeared when, with a pull on the reins, the young woman— she was about twenty-four or -five, Meli thought— wheeled her mount and rode off at a fast pace without speaking.

When the other woman was out of sight, Meli turned back to cross the brook and go to the house, feeling foolish about the brief encounter . . . as if she had tried to hold a conversation with a mirage.

Paula was on the enclosed gallery when Meli climbed the steps and went inside. Meli was glad to have someone to talk to who responded.

"You are an early riser," Paula commented. She poured a glass of juice for each of them and handed one to Meli.

"It's the fishing camp influence. I get up at four

o'clock during the season to open the bait house. I used to," she amended. "Now the Robinsons take care of that part of the operation."

"How does it feel to have free time?" Paula asked curiously.

Meli considered. "Nice," she decided, "but it is hard to turn responsibility over to someone else after doing everything yourself. Do you know what I mean?"

Paula, sipping her juice, nodded. "Tor and I were talking about that last week. He said he wants to lighten his load so that he won't have to be on the road as much. He said he was ready to distribute the workload among his managers and take more time for himself. I think that will be good, don't you?"

"Yes, of course," Meli said, thinking of his offer to spend more time with her this summer.

A picture of the young woman on the next estate galloped into her thoughts and refused to leave. She saw the graceful hands on the reins, hands that wouldn't so much as lift in a greeting.

Meli glanced at her own hands cupped around the juice glass on the table. Her fingers, too, were long and slender, almost delicate in appearance. But capable, she thought. And in her youth she had had slight calluses on her palms, thanks to her girl-scout days of canoeing and camping.

Comparing the two words, callus and callous, she considered a toughness of the hands to be better than a toughness of the heart. And how else did you describe a person who looked you over from her superior height, then rode off as if you didn't exist? For some reason, the incident bothered her more than she cared to admit.

"Miss O'Connor?"

Her attention was brought back to the present by James. He inquired again about her preference for breakfast. Tor came in while she was thinking and ordered Western omelets for both of them.

"Bring her a lot. She eats like a lumberjack," he teased.

His gaze took in her bare feet and the pants rolled up to her knees. "What have you been doing this morning?" he asked after the butler disappeared into the house.

Giving him a cheeky grin, she said, "Exploring. Wading in your creek. It's much warmer than mine. In fact, it's very nice here."

"You like it?" he asked quickly.

"Yes."

"As much as your mountains? We don't have all that rugged grandeur you're used to . . ." His voice trailed into a question.

"It has a charm all its own," she hastened to assure her host and hostess, as two pairs of blue eyes watched her. "Each place does, if you take the time to find it. New York was unique with its sense of *happening*. And I loved Central Park, the library, the theaters . . . and the ferries."

"And here?" Tor asked softly.

"You have a sense of serenity. The rolling terrain is so green, it gives the impression of a nurturing place . . ."

"A nurturing place," Paula murmured. "I like that."

Meli's glance at Tor found his warm gaze on her, and she felt deliciously happy for no particular reason. The episode with the strange female next door receded to the far corners of her mind as the conversation became general. For the next hour, the three of them ate, then relaxed over coffee and talked.

"How was the dance last night? Did you meet any men you thought might be possibilities?" Paula asked.

Meli shrugged. "I don't know. Tor introduced me to about four dozen people in the space of two hours, jostled me around the dance floor about three times, and brought me home."

While Paula laughed, Tor looked aggrieved. "I do not jostle!" he protested. "And I couldn't help it if there were a lot of people present that I knew. They all wanted to know who you were. That's why they kept stopping at our table or talking to us while we danced."

Meli's nervousness last night had lasted only through the first introduction, and she chatted easily, if briefly, to the people she had met.

What Tor said about everyone wanting to meet her was true. They had been swamped by other guests. She had recognized the curiosity that had brought other people to them. When Tor introduced her as his houseguest, she had watched the interested speculation appear in the other people's eyes.

When he added, "She and my cousin are staying the month with me," she saw their assessment change from "mistress" to "friend of the family." It had been amusing.

Although she had enjoyed going to the country club, she admitted the main reason for her pleasure in the evening was Tor. He had gone all out to be the perfect host, full of light quips and innocent stories about the various people she met. She had not particularly liked the other guests at first.

They were what she had come to call the "hard-core partygoers." Her former husband had been one, so it was easy for her to recognize the type. Bored and restless, with no inner life, they lived from one gathering to the next, always on the go. Or they were plagued with a blind ambition to get to the top, to be seen in all the right places.

Of course, not everyone was like that. Some people did go to parties because they enjoyed a change of scene and liked to see their friends in a more relaxed environment, but they were selective about the social events they chose to attend. Tor and Paula belonged to this last group.

Her thoughts turned to Tor. Why did he take her to that dance? she wondered. Just to have it known who she was? He had kept her moving so much that all anyone would have been able to find out was her name and the fact that she was his guest.

Paula interrupted with a request. "Would you go back to the creek and let me sketch you wading in the water? I'd like to do a study—"

"Not a chance. You can have her during the day when I'm at the office, but the evenings and weekends are mine," Tor declared possessively. He turned to his blushing guest. "How's your tennis?"

"I know how to play, but I tend to hit everything out of the court."

"We'll work on that, then. Get your shoes and racket," he ordered. "I have a couple of calls to make. Meet you here in . . ." He glanced at his watch. "Thirty minutes. Okay?"

When he left, Paula grabbed her sketch pad and drew a quick study of Meli in her tousled state. Later, when Meli and Tor went to the tennis court at the side of the house, Paula went to her room to work.

"She's really good, isn't she?" Meli mused, swinging along beside his tall form.

Tor opened the screened gate into the court. "Yes, she is. I'd like her to do a full portrait of you for me."

She was disturbed by his suggestion. Stopping by the net, she clutched the support post with a cold hand. "You must have a thousand photos of me. Why clutter up the place with a portrait? If you marry—*when* you marry—your wife might not want it around." Her grin was saucy. "I won't let my husband keep a painting of an old lover!" She was emphatic.

"I'll remember that," he said cryptically. "Come on, let's see what you can do."

They hit the ball back and forth until he saw where she needed help, then he advised her on her swing.

For an hour he instructed her in a friendly, noncritical manner.

"You'd make a good teacher," she said, praising him.

"Uh-huh," he agreed with no trace of modesty.

After the lesson, they played a set at a leisurely pace. As she tired and her return became more erratic, he made exaggerated leaps to get impossibly high-flying balls, which made her laugh and finished her game entirely.

"I give up!" she yelled, walking toward the gate.

Tor dropped an arm over her shoulders as they returned to the house. "That was fun, wasn't it? We have always laughed at the same things," he mentioned casually. He was smiling, but his eyes, as he looked down on her, were serious. The heightened color in her cheeks could have been caused by the exertion of the game.

Meli went to her room to bathe and change clothes. The two short dresses purchased the previous day were hanging in her closet. That had been fast. Tor probably wanted her to wear one of them for the dinner guests that evening. But she had her own plans.

Meli's eyes instinctively went to Tor's face when she entered the living room that evening. She watched his eyes widen slightly as he observed her. She stopped next to the drinks trolley where he was mixing martinis.

The clinging knit she wore was of lustrous silk in a deep plum color that made her eyes appear to have a violet hue. The dress was sleeveless but had a cape that fitted smoothly over her shoulders and was just long enough to reach her elbows.

"What a stunning color." Paula came over from the sofa to finger the material as she admired the shimmering hue. "I think I'm jealous," she said, eyeing her own black faille skirt and print blouse.

"Thank you," Meli said modestly. With a quick glance from under her lashes at Tor, who was still admiring her with his eyes, she added, "This is my afternoon-into-evening frock. It took me months to find just what I wanted. I have a lace jacket I can wear with it, too." She turned the full brilliance of her smile on him. His pained expression told her the little barb had gone home.

"A thousand apologies, my fair lady." He pressed a hand to his heart and bowed gallantly.

"What was that for?" Paula wanted to know. She accepted the offered martini.

Meli took the glass he handed her. "Mr. Halliday didn't think my wardrobe was up to his standards," she replied nonchalantly.

"You mistook my meaning, Miss O'Connor. Your taste in clothes has always been impeccable. It was the quantity of them that was in question."

When his smooth explanation ended, Meli pretended to consider. At last she said, "But how could you be sure of my taste? You've only seen me in jeans, I think."

Tor raised his glass in salute. "Your jeans have always been in the very best of taste," he solemnly declared. With a perfectly straight face, he added,

"Even that pair with the hole in the seat had a certain . . . umm . . . air about them."

They burst into laughter in a three-way tie, and smiles lingered on their faces when James announced the dinner guests.

Mr. Grainger was gaunt. His white hair was thin on top and worn short over the ears, so that the gauntness of his face was unrelieved. His wife was small and rather plump, with warm brown coloring and a bright expression. She reminded Meli of a wren.

Tor introduced his cousin and then turned to Meli. "And this is Meli O'Connor from Montana. She's visiting with us."

"Montana!" Mr. Grainger was surprised into exclaiming. His gray eyes darted from Meli's startled face to Tor's smiling one. "Oh, uh, Montana," he said, recovering his poise. "Lovely place."

Meli pasted a smile on her face and hastily began a conversation with the puzzled Mrs. Grainger on the merits of the southern spring compared to a northern one. She knew that the woman's husband had made the obvious connection between herself and Tor's many trips to Montana.

At the dinner table Paula took the hostess's chair at the end of the table, while Mrs. Grainger and Meli sat on either side of Tor. Mr. Grainger sat on Meli's left between her and Paula.

Before James served the first course, he poured wine for each of them. Meli glanced at him, a slight question in her eyes, but he only smiled blandly. When he left the room, Tor lifted his glass. His glance flashed over the group with real pleasure, but his gaze lingered longest on Meli.

"This is a little premature, but since we're all family, so to speak, I give you"—Tor held his glass toward Mr. Grainger—"SCL's vice-president and general manager of the New York Division."

Amid the exclamations, Meli caught Tor's slight wink. She was warmed all the way through. So he had found a place for the older man in his main company after all. She was glad, and so were the older couple, judging by their faces.

"Does this mean you'll live in New York?" she asked.

"Yes," Mr. Grainger said. "Dolly's family lives there, so it will be a homecoming for her."

"Why, how wonderful!" Meli was delighted with the news. She smiled at Dolly Grainger, then turned to Tor. "Did you know that?"

He shrugged modestly. "I think Stan had mentioned the fact. However, it wasn't a deciding factor." That remark drew general laughter. All of them knew the boss of SCL promoted only on the basis of merit.

The announcement set the tone of the evening, which passed swiftly with an equal mix of light and serious conversation. Tor and Stan Grainger explained the new corporate structure that would be officially disclosed Monday at the regular staff meeting of the corporate officers.

Meli learned that Paula was on the board of the corporation.

"I had an investment in the manufacturing firm

that my uncle started. When Tor took over, he insisted that I get involved."

"Women should know what their money is doing," Tor stated. "It doesn't take that much effort to learn something about business." He nodded toward Meli. "This woman is one of the best managers I've ever encountered. She knows how to plan and carry through. Many people can do the first; the second part is the hardest."

Meli stifled the rush of euphoria that went to her head faster than the wine she had drunk.

Dark blue eyes pierced her bubble of happiness as he continued. "Of course, sometimes she gets a little carried away with her grand schemes. That's when she needs a good supervisor to keep her in line."

She assumed an outraged pose. "I assume you consider that part of your job, to keep others in line," she challenged.

He gestured arrogantly. "Of course."

"Humph!" she snorted inelegantly. She crossed her arms over her chest, and the light of battle entered her eyes.

"Shall we go into the living room?" Paula interposed hastily, relieved when Tor and Meli rose and quietly followed her out.

It was much later when the Graingers said good night and left. Paula immediately excused herself and went off to bed.

"Well, that was nice," Meli admitted. She pivoted to say good night to Tor and found him standing right beside her.

"Yes, it was," he said in deep tones whose meaning she knew so well.

"Well, good night." She started to flee.

"Don't go," he requested softly. His hand touched her shoulder but fell back to his side at once.

Her insides contracted into tight bands. "I really should . . ."

"Yes, you should," he agreed harshly, bringing her eyes back to his. "Because if you stay, I'll probably end up breaking my word. I want to make love to you." His tone gentled. "Very much, Meli. Very, very much."

"Don't, please," she pleaded.

"Don't what? Don't say it or don't try it? Run on to your empty bed, little girl, or it will be impossible not to try."

"Tor!" She drew a ragged breath, not sure what she was going to say.

"Go on!" he gritted, striding over to the coffee table and picking up his unfinished drink. He downed the rest of it in one gulp. With a crash, he set it back on the polished surface and turned on her angrily. "Go!"

She fled to her room, not stopping until she was inside with the door locked behind her.

Anger erupted like a tidal wave in her. How dare he act like that toward her! She ought to go tell him exactly what she thought of his boorish manners. . . .

But not while he was in the throes of his own temper.

She reflected on how abruptly his mood had changed as soon as they were alone. She certainly understood his frustration, knowing it had been building all evening. She had felt some of the same frustration as she sat beside him for hours, sharing food and laughter and companionship.

She now knew exactly what to tell Tor if he made any derogatory remarks about her wish to get married again. This evening had been a prime example of what she was missing in her life.

Sure it was fun and exciting to have a lover from far away who dropped in bringing crazy gifts, made mad love to you, and then took off again, but it wasn't enough. Those visits were episodes, not a full life.

She put on the midnight blue gown and her robe. While she was washing her face and brushing her teeth, she considered the problems of marriage. All married couples had disagreements that were unresolved. In those cases, it was better to agree to disagree and then get on with the day-to-day living. But she thought most difficulties could be solved by working together. *Together*, that was the operative word.

She turned out the light, walked over to the doors opening out on the garden, and went out. Standing at the end of the roofed patio, she emptied her mind of everything but the enjoyment of moonlight casting black and silver shadows over the landscape. It was not unlike the small, wild meadows of her home.

A sort of homesickness gripped her at the thought and she clenched her fists helplessly at her sides, no longer sure what she wanted. For a moment she wanted to be back in her cabin, to have Tor come striding in and grab her up into his strong arms . . .

The thought conjured up the man. She saw him stroll toward the house from the direction of the side lawn. The swimming pool was over there, she had discovered that morning. Had Tor been swimming at this hour?

He stopped on the flagstone path, and she could see that he was wearing a robe of dark terrycloth. His hair, still wet, was plastered sleekly to his head. She shrank into the shadows as she saw him raise his head and look toward her room.

For several minutes she was almost afraid to breathe while he stood there staring with longing written in every line of his tense form. Her heartbeat was so loud she was sure he would hear it and know of her presence. Maybe he did. He was looking directly at the spot where she stood concealed. With an angry swing of his shoulders, he pivoted and walked off.

Meli crept silently into her room, closed and locked the outside doors, and crawled into bed. Her hands were shaking.

If she wasn't careful, she was going to fall in love with him all over again as she had that summer they had met. Her breath caught in horror at what she was thinking.

No, her shocked mind shouted. No. She wouldn't go through that again.

She had been in the process of falling more and

more deeply in love with her golden lover from the South until she had called his home that time. Talking to Mary Beth had brought her up against the hard truth: Tor was not in love with her and she wasn't special to him—not at that time.

It had taken several days of calm rationalizing to bring the thing into the proper perspective and convince her foolish heart that what she felt was a deep friendship. But that had finally come about. Tor was her very best friend. Friendship and passion, that's what they had shared. The fact that she now wanted more was the reason she was looking for a husband. Slowly, as she talked this over with herself, her emotions calmed and she grew sleepy.

Sunday morning was one of those perfect days of spring that poets write about. There was just enough breeze to be pleasant whether one was sitting in the shade sketching as Paula was doing or lying in the sun by the pool as Meli was. Tor was swimming laps up and down the rectangular pool.

Again Meli had been the first one up that morning. She had drunk a glass of juice and made coffee, feeling like a sneak thief in the immaculate and modern kitchen. Then she had laughed at herself. There was no reason for her not to be as relaxed in Tor's home as he was in hers.

When he came into the gallery for breakfast, he had cast her one penetrating glance that seemed to search out her soul; then he had smiled and resumed the attitude of indulgent parent to wayward daughter that he had assumed with her at the dance Friday night.

That attitude had disappeared by the time he heaved himself out of the water beside her, droplets spraying on her sun-warmed tummy and giving her a chill.

"Nothing works," he said.

Placing an arm over her forehead to shade her eyes, she opened them and looked at him with a bland expression. She didn't ask what he meant, but he explained anyway.

"I swam last night. I swam just now. I still want you." His eyes raked down her body, then returned to her face in accusation. "Do you realize what seeing you in that bikini does to me? Or do you care?"

"Yes, I care," she said softly. She glanced at Paula, but she was working on a drawing of the lawn and trees.

His gaze became fierce. Then he sighed heavily. "For some reason I didn't think it would be this difficult, but seeing you, knowing you really belong to me . . ."

"I don't!" she said sharply, catching Paula's attention. Meli smiled weakly and the artist returned to her task.

". . . not being allowed to touch you." He laid a flat palm on her bare abdomen, watching her closely as he did.

Sitting up, Meli removed his hand, placed it on his thigh, and quickly drew back. "You promised, Tor.

You gave me your word not to try anything while I was here," she whispered in a rising temper. Didn't he think it was hard on her, too? Was he the only one with feelings?

Turning from her, he pulled one knee up and leaned on it with his arms crossed. Several fleeting emotions passed over his features. "I said I wouldn't seduce you . . . physically," he agreed. A half smile curved his mouth. "But I did say I was going to try to change your mind." His direct look at her was startling. She felt as though she had been dazzled by a piece of sky falling.

"I have news for you, my friend. I am not going to change my mind!" The tilt of her head was haughty.

"Not even after last night?" he inquired in a silky voice.

"What do you mean?"

"You had as hard a time going to sleep as I did."

So he had seen her. "My feelings run as deep as yours. You should know that better than anyone." She raised one shoulder and dropped it, proud of her cool control.

"Your passion," he corrected. "I know your passion runs deep, but about your other feelings, I don't know. Friendship can mean different things."

As Meli started to rise, needing very desperately to get away from his disturbing gaze and conversation, Paula protested.

"Don't move," she called with such pleading in her voice that Meli stayed. Glancing across the patio, she saw Paula's pencil moving with rapid strokes across the pad as the artist captured the couple sitting beside the pool.

Tor's grin was sardonic. "Trapped," he said, seeing Meli's predicament.

Meli shook her head. "Not at all. I'm my own person and I can handle whatever you say to make me want you," she said with dramatic emphasis. Then she reached out a lazy hand and stroked from his throat down over his lightly bronzed chest to the waistband of his black swimsuit.

"You're playing with fire," he warned, eyes flashing.

She laughed beguilingly, dropping her head back and moving her shoulders forward in a deliberate, provocative manner. "You promised to keep your hands off me; I didn't promise to keep mine off you," she murmured. She watched his reaction with half-closed eyes full of amusement.

"By heavens, woman . . ."

"Be still, Tor. Please," Paula wailed from behind them.

It delighted Meli to make him lose his control. He was too often in charge of all interaction between them; she loved having a little power now and then.

When Paula finished, James brought their lunch out. Then it was time to get ready for the art show and tea party.

"I'll take you out to dinner after the show," Tor told Meli, belatedly glancing at his cousin to include her in the invitation.

"You two go on without me," she said. "I'll drive in on my own."

"I'll come home with you," Meli stated.

"You'll both go out to dinner with me," Tor thundered, sounding very much like his namesake.

Meli and Paula looked at each other. "Yessir," they said in unison.

Chapter Eight

M eli was supremely conscious of Tor's lean body next to her as he drove down Peachtree Street. His silvery gray suit was an effective foil to the blue dress she wore, the one he had bought for her. She also wore a hat and neat white gloves. Paula, in the back seat, was similarly dressed.

The poolside conversation replayed constantly through Meli's mind. Tor's admission that he considered her to be his didn't make her feel any better. Like him, she found that this visit was harder than she had anticipated.

It had been a stupid idea. He had been right about that, too. She would look for a husband in her own neck of the woods. That was the only practical thing to do.

It was equally foolish to have involved her lover in the quest, she mused discontentedly. She should have broken off with him and started fresh. That was easy to see now.

They stopped at a traffic light. There were people on the street, but not as many as there had been on Friday. Sunday was a quiet day in the city as well as in the country.

A penny landed in her lap.

Glancing over at Tor, she met his laughing glance. He seemed in good spirits this afternoon.

"Worth more than that?" he asked, indicating the coin.

Smiling, she shook her head. "Save your money. You wouldn't care to hear my thoughts."

"Try me," he invited softly, his voice a rippling of mountain water over smooth green stones.

"I was thinking about finding my husband," she answered truthfully enough. Expecting a hardening of his expression, she was surprised when he grinned.

"Yes, that is a thought-provoking subject. One that deserves much consideration. . . ." The words trailed off into a suggestive silence.

Meli, not sure of his meaning, spoke firmly. "Yes, I'm giving it very careful consideration."

He laughed out loud as the light changed and the car moved off smoothly. What was so funny?

The beginnings of anger unfurled in her middle before she decided not to let him ruin her day. This might be the day she would meet Prince Charming.

Who knows? She returned her former lover's laugh with a benign smile of confidence.

Tor parked in a private lot across the street from the art gallery where the exclusive showing was to be held. The attendant gave them a ticket which Tor tossed into his car before locking it. Then they crossed the street.

"I'm very excited about this showing," Paula murmured, taking Meli's arm and giving it a squeeze.

"Do you know the artist?" she asked.

"Yes, he used to be my husband."

Meli stopped in her tracks. "Your husband!"

"Mm-hmm." Paula urged her on and they crossed to the door, which Tor gallantly opened for them. "Artistic jealousy and all that," she said, succinctly explaining the failure of her marriage. "I was a success and he wasn't."

"Oh," Meli said faintly.

"I do hope this show is a smash. It would be so good for his ego—not to mention his pocketbook." Paula giggled softly.

Inside, they stopped to peruse the quietly elegant room. Several people milled about talking in small groups, their tones hushed as if they were in church.

Paula lowered her voice to whisper to Meli, "That's Livingston over there, the one with the auburn hair. Next to him is the gallery owner, the small, older man. His name is Art Brys. His real name is Bryschefski, but no one can remember it so he just chopped off the last part." Paula grinned impishly. "Art did well with Livingston; he got him into a suit."

"Is he a jeans-and-smock artist?" Meli asked.

Paula nodded. "That was one of our problems when we were married. My money interfered with his image of himself as the starving artist. He felt one should *suffer* for one's art." She waved a hand toward a corridor of the gallery. "That side over there contains work done mostly during our marriage. When you look at it, you'll know he suffered a lot at that time . . . in spite of my money. Oh, that brunette hovering on the fringe is the latest mistress."

"Paula!" Art Brys came forward with both hands extended. Paula bent forward so the small, impeccably dressed gallery owner could kiss her on each cheek.

During the introductions, Meli responded politely, then let her attention wander across the room to the artist, Livingston Haley. She had checked his last name on the program Mr. Brys had given her. Paula used her maiden name now just as Meli did. She saw no reason to hang on to a name bestowed in marriage when that marriage no longer existed, especially when there were no children.

When they drifted over and met Livingston, Meli noted that there was no trace of bitterness or jealousy, either artistic or personal, in Paula's manner. She was cordial to both her former husband and his mistress.

Livingston and Paula immediately launched into a

discussion of the show that left Tor, Meli, and Jeanette, the mistress, out. With a murmured excuse, Jeanette went to greet someone she knew, and Art tore himself from the discussion to follow her and welcome the newcomers.

"Shall we make the grand tour?" Tor invited, holding out a hand to Meli. Tucking her hand into the crook of his arm, he guided her along one wall where paintings of park scenes were attractively displayed.

"I like these," Meli said, stepping into a little alcove of sketches that showed how the artist had arrived at some of his final pictures. She found this aspect of the work informative; it also increased her interest in the paintings themselves. "He is a good artist, isn't he?" She glanced up at her silent companion.

Tor nodded as he turned from a sketch of a rabbit sitting at attention in some tall grasses. "He's not a good prospect, though. Poor husband material."

Meli thought that was funny. "I assure you I didn't consider him for a minute."

"Well, famous artist and all that," he mused. "Women seem to go for that sort of thing. Now what I have in mind for you is someone a little more stable, someone who would be able to control your wilder impulses."

Meli held the smile on her face, but inside she was in a fine rage. "That sounds just like what I had in mind too," she agreed sweetly.

"How often would you say you get these notions?

Let's see, you married at twenty-one, were married for five years, and now you want to get married again three years later. So, about every three to five years, I'd say, your husband would have to be prepared to head you off from some escapade."

"You make me sound like a runaway mare who has seized the bit." She removed her hand from his arm.

Tor held out his hand and studied it thoughtfully. The broad palm showed calluses at the base of each finger. "Yes, a man would need a firm hand, I think. We'll have to keep that in mind along with the other traits. Firm hand, likes kids, great in bed . . ." He began numbering them off on his fingers.

A woman standing behind him gave a startled exclamation and darted on past the alcove.

"Oh, sorry," Tor murmured at her departing back, not at all repentant. Meli couldn't help giggling. He gave her a crooked grin and pulled her along to the next grouping, which were oval-framed caricatures of famous people. They spent several minutes identifying the faces of actresses, statesmen, news commentators, and TV personalities before moving on.

"He really is talented," she said, looking at a life-size portrait of Jeanette, who seemed strangely mature and pensive in the painting.

"And a contradiction." Tor nodded toward the mistress. "She comes from a wealthy family. He acts as if he despises money, yet he's always attracted to those who have it."

He was interrupted by the arrival of Paula. "May I borrow Tor for a few minutes, Meli? I have some business to discuss with him and Art about a New York showing, if you don't mind."

"I'll be fine," Meli said.

After the cousins hurried off to join Art and another man, then disappear into a side room, Meli glanced around at the people at the show. She was really more interested in them than in the paintings.

Livingston Haley was the focal point, of course. He was a little taller than she, neither handsome nor ugly. A smattering of gray highlighted his auburn hair, which waved back from his broad forehead in a thick mane. He looked like a visiting fireman, she thought, middle-aged and going to seed.

Going around an end partition, she strolled up the corridor containing his earlier work. These were rough, full of rage and confusion, a young man's nightmares. She was filled with pity.

Standing before one particularly violent scene with slashing streaks of red, she shuddered. It was so angry. She glanced at the date and wondered if it had been done during the time his marriage was coming apart.

A smile brightened her somber features as she stood before a sketch of something that looked like a space-age steam engine excavating a hole in blue dirt.

A conspiratorial whisper sounded near her right ear. "What do you think it is?"

Meli glanced over her shoulder into gray eyes.

Their owner was a man, attractive, and about six one. He had on a tweed jacket with leather elbow patches and held an unlit pipe in one hand. A college professor, she decided, early forties.

"I don't know," she whispered in the same vein. "We would have to ask the artist or an engineer."

The man waved his pipe. "I teach in the engineering department at Georgia Tech. Haven't the foggiest idea what the contraption is."

So she had guessed correctly about his occupation. Feeling a little smug, she studied the next painting; the professor ambled along beside her. This one looked like red ketchup falling on a casserole of green earthworms. "Ugh," she said.

"My feelings exactly!" His chuckle was very pleasant. "My name is William Smith Jordache, by the way."

"As in jeans?" she asked.

"No connection, unfortunately." His slight shrug expressed some regret at not being attached to the clothing fortune.

"I'm Meli O'Connor. From Montana," she added for no reason.

"What brings Meli O'Connor from Montana to our fair city?"

She liked the way he said her name, in a friendly but not intimate way. He was interested but not pushy. For a moment she debated with herself about telling him the truth, but discretion won out over a mischievous streak. "I'm a houseguest of Tor Halliday and his cousin, Paula."

"Halliday, huh?" The gray eyes narrowed.

"You know him?"

"I had him in a class once when I was teaching and working on my doctorate. He has an undergraduate degree in mechanics, I believe."

"Yes, that's right."

"Paula is in from the country, you said?" His expression changed when he spoke of the woman, becoming friendly once more.

"Yes, she and I are visiting at Tor's home this month." She wondered why he didn't like Tor.

"Then perhaps we shall see each other again." He smiled at her, letting her see his definite interest. "I insist on it. Are you free any day this week?"

"I'm not sure," she began hesitantly. "I know we're going to the concert Friday night and to a ball on Saturday."

"Then we will meet again. I'll be looking forward to it." Tipping his pipe to her, he gracefully took his leave. He stopped to speak to Livingston on his way out, then gave her a smiling glance over his shoulder at the door.

Meli left the depressing drawings and returned to the main showing, liking his later work much better. The artist had matured a lot over the years. She walked down a row she hadn't seen, gasping when she came to two identically framed portraits. One was of the artist; under his hand was a globe of the world, and next to him a window looked out on distant vistas. It was titled *Prizes Gained*. Next to it was a picture of Paula; its name: *Prizes Lost*.

She was still standing there when Tor returned. Her eyes were haunted. "What does it mean? That he gained the world and lost his love? Was love the price he had to pay for his art?"

"I don't know, Meli." He spoke with feeling. "I guess only he can answer that."

He led her into another room where Paula stood next to a table of refreshments, talking with Jeanette. Both women appeared happy with the showing of Livingston's work. Sipping from a glass of champagne Tor had given her, Meli listened to the discussion concerning the practical side of the affair. There had already been several sales and commissions for new work. Apparently the young mistress handled the business side of the show, and she spoke with Livingston's former wife about it.

"He's had several offers for the *Prize* pictures, but, of course, we won't let them go," she said.

"Oh, no, he shouldn't," Paula agreed. "They are by far his best work. I've talked to Tor and Art about New York."

Meli puzzled over the women's attitude until she noticed Tor's glance. He leaned over to her. "Artists are confusing people, aren't they?"

"Definitely!"

He laid a hand on her arm and tugged her over to one side. "Now you and I are very much alike. We tend to know what we want and go after it, no holds barred."

Her brows rose slightly at this assertion. He was implying that she was as ruthless as he was. "I don't think that's a virtue. I admire Paula for the way she's trying to help. It seems . . . ennobling. I think it shows character to be able to remain friends and help each other after a breakup."

"Would you help your ex?"

Meli's eyes dropped from Tor's gaze. She grimaced. "I frankly doubt it. I wouldn't hurt him, I don't think, but I wouldn't go out of my way for him either."

Tor's fingers brushed a curl lying against her temple. He laughed lightly. "See? We're two of a kind."

His hand slipped along her jaw and pressed under her chin to lift her face to his. She recognized the message he was sending and knew he had started the campaign of verbal seduction he had promised.

"You look beautiful," he said. "Thank you for wearing my dress."

Meli had to join in his laughter at the wording. "It does fit me better than it does you," she teased.

Walking with her to the refreshment table, he inquired innocently, "Did you notice how often we laugh together?"

Tor stayed by her side the remainder of the afternoon. It was dark when they returned to the car. Paula chatted happily about the good turnout as they drove along winding streets to the restaurant where they had reservations for dinner.

Meli relaxed in the comfortable seat, realizing that she could easily fall asleep. She felt a tantalizing sensation on her wrist. Glancing down, she discovered Tor's fingers tracing circles along the sensitive inner skin, making it tingle. She slapped his hand away. "Don't touch."

He glared at the errant hand. "I don't know how that happened," he declared.

"Just watch it," she warned.

"I will, I certainly will," he promised fervently.

Paula leaned forward. "What's going on up there?"

"A private battle," Tor replied, smiling at his drowsy companion, who was stifling a yawn.

His cousin chuckled as she settled back into the upholstery. "You two have a good relationship. You remind me of Livingston and myself. Of course it took us thirty years to arrive at it," she said ruefully.

"I've tried to tell her," he said, not the soul of tact. "But she won't listen. Thinks she needs a husband when actually we have it all already. Laughter, companionship, great . . ."

Meli's breath got tangled in her throat and she couldn't say a word.

". . . sense of adventure," he concluded.

As they pulled into a parking lot she gave him a look that promised revenge.

The restaurant Tor had selected was on a hill. A trickle of water ran over rocks along the side of the hill, forming a delightful little pool at the bottom. A willow and cane thicket grew over the area.

"How attractive!" Meli exclaimed.

"I knew you'd like it." Tor's voice was deep, vibrant.

As they sat at a small table in the lounge before going in to dinner, Meli found herself mesmerized by the glowing look in his eyes. She saw the memories from the past reflected in those bottomless depths, knew he was deliberately bringing them to her. She looked away.

It would be so easy to let herself think they were started on a new course in their affair and then to fall back into the old patterns. The only real difference would be that she would come visit him, either here or in New York, instead of his coming to her all the time. She wanted more than that.

People like Livingston Haley probably should never get married. They weren't able to bring the necessary maturity to marriage. They needed mothers to soothe them and take care of problems and to cheer them along.

Meli mulled this over.

Tor wasn't like that. She had heard him on the telephone and knew him to be a powerful, dominant businessman, cool and capable in his dealings with others. No woman would have to manage his affairs for him.

Neither did he need a cheerleader. His self-confidence was unshakable. Too much so, she realized, seeing his gaze flick over her again. He had every expectation of putting an end to her "crazy notion." And continuing where they had left off.

He was in for a surprise. She would show him she meant business. Crossing her fingers, she wished William Jordache would show up again and make a play for her. Or she could make a pass at him. These were modern times.

"Just what madcap scheme are you hatching now?" Tor wanted to know. "Don't deny it. I know that look you get." His narrow-eyed scrutiny brought a gurgle of laughter from Meli and Paula.

"Men rarely know half what they think they do," Paula said, defending her sex by attacking his. "Isn't that right, Meli?"

"Precisely!" She stirred the drink that the waitress had brought and gave a superior smile to her escort.

When they went into the dining room, he placed her by his side with a possessive air that earned him another warning from smoky eyes. Smiling, he released her waist from his clasp.

"Sorry," he muttered, not meaning it.

The crust on the beef Wellington was golden brown and flaky, the pâté and mushrooms perfect. The side dish of artichoke hearts was a delicious adjunct to the entree. Meli had to turn down the Black Forest cake with a regretful sigh. She considered asking for a doggie bag so she could eat it as a midnight snack.

"Would you like to dance?" Tor invited still later over coffee.

Paula was sitting at a nearby table, chatting with friends. For someone who claimed to be a semi-hermit, she seemed to have a lot of friends.

Without thinking, Meli nodded and let him take her to the floor. It was there that she realized she had made a mistake. The knowledge dawned in her face right after he took her in his arms. The sexual tension that she had carefully suppressed all day swept over her like a crown fire in a forest of dry timber. She beat it into embers with the force of her will.

Tor was strangely silent as they moved around the dim, crowded space. Was he fighting his own fires?

Her pulse quickened and her eyes went midnight dark as the scent of his cologne wafted around her, mingling with her perfume.

"You smell good," he murmured. "Is that a new perfume? It doesn't smell the same as the one you wear at home." He sniffed delicately below her ear before straightening.

She knew he meant her mountain home. Her voice was slightly husky when she answered. "I don't wear perfume in the mountains. When you live in an area where there are wild animals who eat honey, you don't go around smelling like a honeypot." Her teasing smile was shaky. His nearness was upsetting her. Trying to widen the one-inch gap that separated them, she somehow succeeded in closing it.

He chuckled, and his arms tightened around her.

"Tor!" she warned.

Hands stroked caressively down her back in a soothing motion.

"Don't!"

"Honey, I can't dance with you without touching you," he drawled, sounding very reasonable.

"Keep your hands still!"

"I was just trying to move you out of the way."

Meli was bumped by another couple.

"See?"

"A fake air of innocence does not become a

thirty-four-year-old man, Tor." She was without mercy.

"Ouch! Do I mention your age?" He was wounded but being brave about it.

"You're impossible," she finally declared, giving up trying to reprimand him.

His voice was sexily raspy next to her ear. "Oh, I'm possible, witch; very, very possible where you're concerned."

Both irritation and amusement fled at the sincere longing in his statement.

"Do you realize it's been three weeks since I last held you in my arms? Holding you isn't enough, Meli, not when I've had it all. Is it for you?"

She tried to hold herself stiffly away from his powerful form, but it was a task beyond her ability when his hands molded her so intimately to him. His eyes glittered hotly over her, seeing her dilemma as she fought the hunger between them.

"You promised," she whispered hoarsely.

"All's fair," he quoted. "Don't fight it. Why shouldn't we have this?"

Meli listened to his persuasive words. She gathered her forces and answered him. "Because it wouldn't be fair to my future husband."

Every muscle in his body contracted to steel hardness, and for the first time, she was afraid of him. His blue eyes were fierce with rage. She expected to feel talons closing on her at any minute, but his hands stayed gentle on her back. He inhaled sharply.

With a sigh, he released his breath. "Ah, yes," he murmured, "the husband." One dark brow arched in inquiry. "Have you met anyone you think would be a candidate?"

"Two, actually." She tried to think of some names.

"Who?"

Meli was surprised at his calm tone. She had expected to withstand another siege, but he had himself in hand now, and nothing could ruffle his control.

"One I met back home at a friend's house. He works for the National Park Service and was very nice—"

"Then why are you down here looking?" he interrupted.

"Well, the ranger was only twenty-five. Very mature," she hastened to add, "but still, younger than I am."

Tor was indulgent. "You must overcome these prejudices, my dear. Who was the other?"

"A man I met at the exhibit. Teaches at a local college, I believe." She smiled in relief at thinking of two men.

"Oh, a teacher." Tor dismissed the man. "Not your type, babe. He'd never be able to handle you."

Meli didn't say any more and Tor evidently thought that closed the subject. He rested his cheek against her hair and moved slowly to the dreamy music.

When they returned to the table, Paula introduced Meli to her friends, an older couple and a guest of theirs from Alabama. She would have liked to talk to the young man, who was about her age and interested in her fishing camp, but she never got the opportunity. The conversation raced from subject to subject with no pauses.

It wasn't until they were on their way home that she realized how talkative Tor had been all evening. Pondering this fact, she realized that he had deliberately kept her from having a private discussion with the other guest. Well, it wasn't worth fighting about, she decided, but from now on she would be conscious of what he was doing and better prepared to cope with it.

A little thrill of excitement ran down her spine. It was fun doing battle with him. It would be even more fun to outwit him! That would be hard, but it was possible. She gave him a sideways glance. Very, very possible, my golden eagle, she told him mentally.

He caught her look and he smiled. She was sure he had been making his own plans. So, the battle lines had been drawn and the war games were truly on. "Full speed ahead" would be her motto. She was still considering strategy when they reached the house and went in.

Meli got a glass of milk from the kitchen and joined Tor and Paula in the library where they were having a nightcap.

Tor looked at her milk. "Just what I would have chosen for you," he said, back in the indulgent-father role that, oddly enough, seemed to suit him.

She simply smiled. An arched brow implied that she found it unnecessary to consult his opinion on the matter.

"Thank you for sponsoring Livingston's show in New York," Paula said to her cousin.

He nodded. "It was an opportunity I thought he deserved."

She smiled, patting back a yawn. "Yes. It's been a long time coming for him. He's finally found his forte. He's best at people." She turned to Meli. "Not society portraits, but portraits that are interpretations of personality."

"I understand," Meli said quietly. The challenge was leaving the evening and she was tired.

"Perhaps we could have him paint your future husband to see if he has any bad traits we've overlooked," Tor suggested.

Not understanding the curtain of melancholy that was closing about her, Meli added lightly, "Or we could ask him to do me. Then maybe I would understand myself."

On that note she stood, bid them good night, and thanked both host and hostess for a lovely time. Tor strolled out with her, escorted her to her bedroom, and stopped at the door, all without touching her.

But his liquid gaze was a caress as he looked down at her. "You'll come back to my bed, Meli. I don't intend to let a day pass without telling you how much I want you there." The softly worded promise rested on the night air between them, heavy with portent.

For a moment, overpowered by his total confidence, she believed him, almost lifted her arms to be taken by him. Biting her lip, she realized just how relentless and ruthless he could be in the pursuit of his desires. It was like making a pet of a bear and becoming too confident about controlling it. When it turned wild, one was unprepared.

Except she was prepared. Hadn't she seen through him tonight? His soft laughter pulled her attention back to him.

"I've given you plenty of advance warning," he said. "You can't accuse me of being *unfair* about my intent." With that, he spun and walked away. Meli heard him whistling as he went up the stairs to his room.

Chapter Nine

"Turn your head a little more, just a little, a little . . . that's it! Hold it right there." Paula's hand dropped to her pad and she began sketching rapidly.

Meli raised her brows slightly, afraid to move anything else as the artist had spent over an hour positioning her. "Composing" the picture was what Paula called it.

Today was Wednesday and the women were on their own for two days. Tor had gone to New York early that morning to meet with his executives and to introduce Mr. Grainger as the new boss of that operation.

Meli was glad of the respite. Since she had arrived last week, they had gone out every night. On Monday, Tor had taken the afternoon off and driven over to Stone Mountain on a sightseeing tour with her. She had enjoyed that. They had barely gotten home in time to eat, rest an hour, then get ready for the mayor's reception.

Her lips softened into a smile as she remembered her autocratic host telling her to wear her black skirt. Glancing down at the white peasant blouse and gypsy skirt Paula had found for her to wear for the sitting, she saw instead her long taffeta skirt and the gold lamé top.

"Don't move!"

Meli brought her head back to the correct angle but her thoughts stayed at the reception. The evening had been sponsored by the mayor to tout Atlanta's excellent cultural opportunities. She wasn't surprised when the top city official greeted Tor by name and introduced him to the head of a committee for the arts, who immediately launched into a discussion of future needs. It didn't take second sight to know this was leading to a request for a donation from SCL.

Tor was surprisingly gracious. "Send me the literature and I'll look it over," he had promised. "SCL is very interested in encouraging young people." Then he had whisked Meli and Paula on past the beaming committee chairman.

The evening had flashed by in a daze, at least on Meli's part. As at the country club dance, Tor had introduced her to so many people that she hadn't a chance of remembering them all or of having a quiet conversation. But no one had intimate discussions at these things, she had realized, listening to the drone of voices that surrounded her.

When Paula moved off on her own to talk to friends, Meli stood by herself for a few minutes. Tor was getting her a glass of champagne and had gotten snagged by a buxom lady in the process. Giggling, Meli watched as he tried to ease away, but a hand on his sleeve held him captive.

"Well, bless my soul! Look who it is—our girl from Montana," a boisterous voice called from the crowd.

Startled, she tried to see someone she recognized in the sea of faces. A young man in his twenties finally burst forth and stood in front of her, a big smile wreathing his boyishly handsome features.

"Ta-dum," he sang out, holding out his arms and striding toward her.

He looked vaguely familiar. Had she met him tonight? Going along with his joking, she turned her face and let him plant a big smacking kiss on her cheek. Who was he?

Holding her by her shoulders, the young man looked her over expectantly. Then, "I can tell by that happy glow that you're delighted to see me . . . and that you don't remember me from Adam," he concluded glumly.

"Sorry," Meli said, trying to look contrite.

He bowed elaborately. "Case Hamilton at your service, madam; swordsman, gallant, and raconteur extraordinaire!" he introduced himself. "Uh, we met at the country club last Friday, if you will permit me to refresh your memory. You were the guest of one Tor Halliday?" His glance was inquiring.

"Yes, that's correct." Meli was enjoying the encounter.

Case grimaced. "But I can't remember your name for the life of me," he concluded.

This confession, coming on the heels of his dashing entrance, brought forth peals of laughter from her. Undaunted, he joined in heartily.

"Meli O'Connor from Polebridge, Montana, sire." She daintily held up her skirt and dropped him a curtsy. She felt as if she had just made her first friend—besides Tor and Paula—since coming to Georgia.

Case immediately took her up on her name. With a distinctive lilt, he said, "Meli, light o' me life, I won't be forgetting ye again, me sweet colleen!" He laid a hand on his heart and juggled a leer and a wink across his face.

They laughed together.

Dropping a casual arm around her shoulders, Case questioned her on her visit. When the waiter came by, he grabbed two glasses of champagne and led her over to a window and fresh air.

The two of them compared the merits of their home states. He wanted to come up to the camp as soon as she returned there.

"But we're booked up for the summer," she protested.

"That's all right. I don't need tent space or a cabin. I plan to camp on your doorstep"—he cast

her a sexy glance from his sparkling black eyes—
"until you let me inside."

Meli continued to engage in teasing repartee with
the merry young man. Case's tactics were apparently
the same as Tor's: wear down the opposition with
constant avowals of desire, teasing humor, and an
offhand gallantry that was almost irresistible.

"Oh-oh, I'd better hit the road, honey," Case said
suddenly in the middle of some long, amusing story.
She glanced over her shoulder.

Tor came toward them, an indulgent smile curving
his lips. "So this is where you got to," he said
equably. "Hello, Case, thanks for entertaining my
guest. I have some people for her to meet now."

Meli was warm in her thanks to Case for a
pleasant time. She waved goodbye over her shoulder
as Tor firmly escorted her across the room. "He was
so nice," she gushed.

Her praise stopped abruptly when Tor's eyes
glittered over her in molten fury. She recoiled from
it.

"We're going home," he said in calm tones.
"Paula is coming later with friends."

They threaded their way through the huge room,
saying their farewells to various groups as they went.
Tor's hand was like a talon on her arm the whole
time. When they went out to the car, she spoke up.
"You're hurting me."

His hold loosened. In a tense silence, he put her
into his car and drove off on the rather long trip back
to his house. Meli began to get angry.

"Just what social blunder have I made that I must be taken home in disgrace?" she asked haughtily.

His face hardened. "I didn't take you to the damned thing just to have you go off in a huddle with the most notorious playboy in Atlanta. That's the second time you've allowed yourself to be picked up by some unknown male . . ."

"Just what does that mean, the second time?" she demanded, her hands clenching on the small purse in her lap.

"Yesterday it was the schoolteacher," he reminded her. "Last night it would have been that kid from Alabama if I hadn't been right beside you to keep an eye on things."

She was so angry she thought she would explode. "How fortunate," she murmured scathingly.

"You'd better watch yourself. You'll end up with a reputation of being a desperate old maid or else an easy mark."

"Thank you very much for your kind advice," she said with acid sweetness. "Don't think I don't appreciate it . . . because I don't!" She nearly shrieked the last words. "You arrogant toad! Who do you think you are to say things like that to me? I can talk to whom I please. You were the one who left me on my own, if you will remember." She huffed out an indignant breath.

His voice was calm, the mature adult reasoning with the tantrum-throwing child. "I'm your best friend. Who else can tell you these things?"

"What things?" she practically shouted.

"You're looking for a husband, right?" he asked.

"I'm rapidly changing my mind. I think a nunnery is sounding better all the time."

He stopped smoothly at a red light. "Honey, that wouldn't suit your nature at all. I know just how you react to a man's caresses." He touched the feathered layers of hair on her neck. She couldn't prevent a shiver, and knew by his fleeting grin that he felt it too. He withdrew, placing both hands on the steering wheel.

"Yes, I melt at the slightest touch from any male," she said bitterly.

He chuckled. "Now I didn't say that. You're choosy, I admit. I'm just trying to help you make the best choice. That's what you asked me to do, wasn't it?"

"No! I only asked you to give me the opportunity to meet some eligible men. I did not ask for your help in selecting them."

The light changed and he moved off, following the dark and winding road. A brisk breeze was shredding the silence with the sighing of leaves.

His voice was so full of understanding that she wanted to hit him. "Maybe not in the actual selection but certainly in the elimination process. I'll save you time by weeding out the bad characters for you. You did say you wanted me to do that, didn't you?"

He waited as she carefully searched the statement for some hidden trap. She didn't trust this helpful Tor—not after he had given her warning that he was going to thwart her plans if possible.

"Case Hamilton is not a possibility, sweetheart." He was so sincere that Meli would have believed him even if she hadn't agreed.

"I never thought he was." She was coolly in control now. "But I want you to know, my *friend,* that I see through your stratagems."

She had the pleasure of seeing his hands, white-knuckled with alarm, jerk on the wheel. "What do you mean?" he asked.

"I know you prevented me from talking to that fellow at the restaurant by directing the conversation. So maybe he wasn't a candidate, either. The question is, when am I going to meet one? At the dinner you're giving tomorrow night?"

He parked the car at the house and helped her out. She always seemed to arrive at this place and time angry or upset.

"No, there won't be any single men there. Just a couple that I happen to like. I went to school with both of them; they're old friends. And Livingston is coming."

"Livingston?"

"Without the mistress."

"My God!" she had been shocked into whispering. As she returned to her room, she had felt as if she would never understand these people. Her view of life was far different from theirs. She realized she was arriving at an understanding of Tor that would have been impossible if she hadn't come to his home, but that didn't alter her own feelings on life and love and marriage . . .

"You can relax now," Paula called, startling her gypsy model back into the present. "Let's have lunch on the patio. Can you sit for a couple of hours this afternoon, too?"

Meli got up, shook out her gypsy skirt, and walked barefoot across the lawn to join the older woman. "Sure," she said.

Over coffee and rolls, they talked about the dinner the previous night with Livingston Haley and the Claytons. Meli had met Milt Clayton the first summer Tor had come to Montana. She had recognized him at once. Milt's wife, Andrea—"Call me Andy," she had said—had the most pronounced Southern accent Meli had heard thus far. It had been difficult to follow the conversation at times.

Then Tor had decided to teach Meli to speak Southern, and that had started them on a hilarious game that lasted the entire evening.

"Did you have a good time? Are you enjoying your visit?" Paula wanted to know.

Meli stretched luxuriously in the webbed lawn chair. "Yes, I did and I am. You and Tor have been simply lovely. And I've enjoyed meeting your friends."

"And ex-husband?" Paula asked with a laugh.

"Livingston is lovely." She contradicted that with a faint giggle. "I don't understand him, but he's lovely."

Before Paula could agree or disagree, James announced a call for Meli.

"For me?" Her heart suddenly went into double time as she followed James into the house and continued into the library to take the call. "Hello?" she said into the receiver.

"Hello, Meli," a baritone voice greeted her. "This is Bill Jordache, the one who's not into jeans? I met you at the art exhibit on Sunday."

"Of course! We did the retrospective tour together. I asked Livingston about that machine and he didn't know what it represented either." Her laughter was joined by his.

"I heard through clandestine rumors"—his voice was very low—"that Tor was out of town for a couple of days. I wondered if you would have dinner with me tonight?"

Meli hesitated. She wasn't sure if she should leave Paula alone.

He seemed to read her mind. "Paula is welcome to come too," he said with a certain dry wit that she liked. She accepted and hung up.

Paula, however, declined to accompany the couple. Bill took Meli to a wonderful restaurant on a steep hill overlooking the highway loop that ran around the city. She had an interesting time, and it was late when he brought her home. In her room, she looked at her mouth in the mirror.

Bill's kiss had been gentle, persuasive, and experienced. Just what she had expected from a forty-year-old man on a first date. It hadn't displeased her, although it hadn't thrilled her, either. Had Tor spoiled her for anyone else? His kisses were so masterful, so exciting. Her breath caught just thinking of his mouth on hers, his lips sliding along her neck, across her breasts. Her nipples thrust against the silk of her nightgown as she pulled it on. The phone rang beside her bed.

"Did you have a good time?" a deeply rippling voice inquired when she answered.

"Yes, I did."

"Where did he take you?" Tor asked.

"Is this an inquisition?" She kept her tone light.

"No," he sighed. "I just called to tell you my bed is big and very comfortable. Also very empty. I wanted you to know."

A frisson swept down her neck. "Thanks."

"No one but you has shared my bed in two years. You know that, don't you?" His voice was husky, as when they made love.

What about Mary Beth? she thought of saying, but didn't. "Do I?" She gave a ghost of a laugh, trying to sound as if his declaration didn't affect her.

"You should." He was suddenly firm with her. "Don't let anyone in yours without telling me first," he ordered.

"Why, you, you . . ." she spluttered, but he had already said good night and hung up. She slammed the instrument down with an unladylike expression.

When he came home the next evening, he made no reference to her dinner date. Bill had refrained from mentioning Tor the previous evening. She wondered what their source of dislike sprang from. Male rivalry?

On Friday night Meli wore the lovely white dress with colorful floral sprays that Tor had bought her.

When she walked into the library, Paula rushed to her. Catching the shining white material between caressing fingers, she exclaimed, "This is it! I want to paint you in this." Her blue eyes danced with excitement. "On the stone fence in the side yard with the pink hedge in the background, present but not dominant . . ."

Tor was plainly disappointed. "Shouldn't it be a nude?" he asked, eyes wide with innocent concern.

"No," his cousin snapped, arranging the folds of the dress, seeing the portrait in her mind already.

"You haven't time to start it now," he reminded them. "We've got to go if we're going to hear the first note of the concert."

Paula prattled on and on about the picture all the way into town. Meli was glad when they were seated inside the auditorium and the music started.

At intermission she freshened up in the lounge and returned to the lobby to find her escorts. A handsome, smiling face with laughing black eyes popped up in front of her. Case opened his arms.

"Meli, me love," he said liltingly, inviting her into his embrace.

"Case!" She let him enclose her in a friendly little hug. "Are you enjoying the concert?"

"It's okay. Mostly I just come to see if there's any new blood," he asserted, peering around lecherously. "Have you escaped your bodyguard? I don't want to get fried in that laser gaze."

She shook her head, hugely enjoying her light-hearted companion. "If you mean Tor, he's my friend, not my guardian," she said. "A kind host," she added for good measure. It was time to return. "Nice seeing you again," she called to him.

"Are you going to the ball tomorrow night?"

"Yes."

His smile promised he would see her there. She hurried over to Tor and Paula, who were looking around for her. She saw Bill Jordache and his date slip into their seats. The woman looked very beautiful from the back, her glossy dark hair piled up in ringlets on her small head.

Tor touched her arm, and when she looked at him, he said, "That's his niece with him."

"I wasn't curious," she retorted. "You two know each other, don't you?" she asked, wondering if it was Paula or James who had told him who her date was the other night. He had known without asking her.

Tor whispered close to her ear, "Sure. We grew up in the same town, went to the same schools."

"Why doesn't he like you?"

He paused to choose his words. "We had a slight disagreement one time, a minor thing," he said, dismissing the problem.

Meli's glance was wise. "Over a woman?"

The lights dimmed, but not before she saw his quick grin and heard his low, "A spoiled brat!"

It wasn't until the three of them were on their way home that he casually asked, "Is Bill Jordache a candidate?"

Meli considered. "Yes, I think so," she said

slowly. "He's the college professor I told you about. The one I met at the art exhibit."

Tor's bark of laughter was unpleasant. "You've chosen well. His family is one of the richest in the state. He could buy and sell me twice over."

"I'm not looking for a bankroll; I want a mate!"

He ignored the outburst. "Bill likes the role of the suave, slightly eccentric professor. Did he have on his coat with the leather patches the other day? And make his points by waving a pipe in your face? I've never seen him smoke the damn thing."

A slight flush colored her cheeks and she was glad it was dark. He made Bill sound like a fake; she didn't like it.

"Don't be petty, love," Paula spoke up from the back. "That's so tacky."

Meli hid a grin at this mild reproach. He had certainly deserved it. Tor clamped his teeth together, and he hardly spoke to either of them until they reached the house and said good night.

The next day Meli woke up early in eager anticipation of the Masque of the Spring Moon Ball, which was to be held that evening. Her new dress hung in her closet. She didn't realize how much she had been looking forward to the event until the last hours before it arrived.

Even the name sounded portentous: Masque of the Spring Moon Ball. She had been to balls before, but none that stirred up such whorls of excitement in her blood.

After taking a scented bath drawn by Mrs. Reynolds that left her feeling like a princess in a fairy tale, Meli carefully removed her earrings and cleaned them. She used her new perfume and powder lavishly before slipping into stockings and lacy underwear.

Mrs. Reynolds returned in time to help her into the evening dress. It looked almost black until the light touched it, and then the material gleamed with blue iridescence, as if it were woven of magic threads.

The strapless bodice fitted perfectly over her breasts, enhancing the gentle cleavage between them. From the snug waist, the silk molded itself to her slender hips like a lover's caress. A translucent shawl was draped around her from neck to ankle.

Mrs. Reynolds withdrew a small case from her pocket. "Mr. Halliday asked that you wear these." She extended the case to Meli and left the room.

With trembling fingers, Meli flipped open the jeweler's box. Inside was a note. "I'd like you to wear these. They belonged to my mother," Tor had written in his bold hand. After fastening the necklace of small diamonds around her throat, she screwed the earrings cautiously into place. Three diamonds dangled from each ear.

Mrs. Reynolds' knock on the door and her reminder of the lateness of the hour caused Meli to hurry. She grabbed her satin purse, pulled the trailing shawl around her, and rushed to join Tor and his cousin.

Paula and Meli admired each other's outfits all the way to the ballroom. The older woman was in pale lavender. Then they pounced on Tor, telling him how handsome he looked in his formal evening clothes.

Flashbulbs went off in their faces when they emerged from the limousine Tor had hired for the evening. The hotel was brilliantly lighted and Meli was glad for her escort's guiding hand as, blinded by all the flashes, she glided across the marble entrance.

They were greeted by the Grand Master of the ball and taken to their reserved seats at a long table. Meli was delighted to see Milt and Andy Clayton already there. They chatted until the opening chords were struck; then Tor led Meli out to join in the first dance. Everywhere she looked there was color and light and the brilliance of jewels and crystal.

"Happy?" he asked.

"Yes," she breathed. "It's like a fairyland. Beautiful, but not quite real."

Looking into his eyes, she felt herself succumbing to the passion that was there for her to see. Not for anyone else, just for her. Other messages were there in those cobalt depths, messages whose meaning she didn't comprehend. Tearing her gaze from him, she watched the swirling figures around her and gave herself entirely to the dance and the moment.

Her heart thudded. It would take only the tiniest nudge for her to fall wildly in love with her charming escort. She could feel it hovering inside her like a bud on the brink of bursting forth in perfect bloom.

What did she want? To love Tor and remain his friend and lover until some vague future time? Could she be satisfied with the crumbs of his affection until he got tired of the effort of seeking her out in her mountain fastness? She knew, in that moment, that she wouldn't come back here or go to New York with him. She wouldn't travel with him as his mistress. She would only meet him where she was his equal—on her home ground.

Later in the evening she danced with Milt Clayton, and then with Livingston when he arrived with his lovely young friend. Finally, Bill came over to their table with his date. Meli caught herself staring and dropped her gaze. The woman was the same one who rode the horse on the estate next to Tor's. She was also the niece from last night. Bill made the introductions.

"Meli, this is my niece. Mary Beth, this is Meli O'Connor from Montana, who is visiting the Hallidays."

Not by so much as a blink did Meli reveal the shock she felt. The younger woman wasn't so disciplined.

"You!" she accused. Then her dark eyes darted to Tor's face, which was drawing into a frown.

"You two have met?" he asked silkily.

"I . . . why, no," Mary Beth denied, increasing Tor's suspicion.

"But you know Meli. How?" He sounded like an inquisitor as he barked the word.

She changed her tactics. Shrugging one bare shoulder, she replied, "It's common gossip that your mistress from Montana is visiting you. I must say I never thought she'd last so long."

The slight pause was charged. "How do you know

how long she's lasted . . . as my mistress or anything else?"

"I . . ." She looked to her uncle for rescue, but he was waiting for her reply too. "I happened to be at your house one time when she called. I, uh, answered the phone."

Meli had to admire the girl's insouciance as she tossed off the answer. She wondered what Tor would do. Surprisingly, he smiled rather grimly at Bill and then led Meli onto the dance floor again.

Taking her into his arms in a smothering embrace, he demanded softly, "Tell me your version of that conversation. It would have been sometime during the summer we met, wouldn't it?"

She would have preferred to forget it, but he wasn't about to let her. "I called to ask your advice on a government form or something. She answered, said you were in the shower, and volunteered to take a message."

"I didn't get your message, Meli."

She was aware that he was thinking the situation over while they danced. He seemed to be considering some facts.

"Meli, I want you to tell me the truth. Was that the reason you never called me or seemed interested in my home during the time I've known you?"

"Part of it," she admitted. "I figured if you wanted me in your life, you would have said something."

His arms tightened around her. "How stupid we've been. I thought you weren't interested. I've always wanted you with me. No matter where I went, it would have been better with you there."

"Don't," she whispered, trying not to hear the seductive call in his voice.

"Listen, I dated Mary Beth some during the spring before I met you, but it was nothing. She started hanging around, coming over uninvited. I finally had to ask her to leave. She went to Bill with a sob story. That's the whole story in a nutshell. There's been no one since you. Not from the very first."

She placed a finger over his lips to silence him, then pulled it away as if burned.

"Touch me," he invited. "I miss your touch. Not a night goes by without my remembering how your hands feel on me."

She hardened her heart against his words, but she had to give him credit for keeping his word. It would be so heavenly to let herself be seduced by the caress in his voice.

"You're so beautiful, Meli. It's driving me out of my mind to know you're thinking of taking another man in my place. You know deep in your heart that you belong to me, that you wouldn't be happy with anyone else."

"What egotism," she mocked lightly.

"I can see the pulse in your throat and I know what it would feel like under my lips, beating so wildly with the passion I can arouse in you." His eyes promised her that passion, and the stars and moon, too.

"I've never denied that you can excite me," she

stated with absolute calm, cursing the pulse that gave her away.

"Let it happen," he pleaded. "One last perfect night to remember."

She felt herself swaying against him. It would be so easy, so very easy to give in to what he wanted . . . what she wanted, too, if she were totally honest. She was being torn into pieces inside. One part of her cried that this was Tor, dearest friend, gentlest lover; while another reminded her that she had set her steps on the path of a different future.

Right now, with his arms so warm around her, with his words so sweet in her ears, she was tempted to slip back into the past and resume their relationship. She stopped that line of thought. Shoring up the crumbling foundation of her decision, she forced herself to concentrate on the dance.

Glancing around, she saw Case's eyes on her. He winked. Wrinkling her nose, she grinned at him.

His flirting reminded her of Mary Beth's accusation. Did everyone in Atlanta think she was Tor's mistress? Why? They had acted very circumspectly in public, and Paula was with them most of the time. So why would people think that?

Of course, right now Tor was acting like a lover. He held her crushed in his arms, his whispered, impassioned demands stirring her with longing.

"Stay with me tonight, sweet witch, and I promise we'll find our special magic."

Meli pushed herself away from him and stared into his smoldering eyes. "We've already had our last night," she reminded him.

Chapter Ten

His smile was confident. "Wanna bet?" he challenged. And when she didn't answer, "Scared?"

"Not at all. Uninterested," she declared.

That brought an uninhibited shout of laughter from him, startling some of the dancers around them. She maintained an aloof, dignified silence until they returned to their table.

After that, Meli danced with other people from the group that drifted around Tor and Paula from time to time. She drank champagne and ate various tidbits that were delicious, the best being a pastry puff filled with a ham mixture.

Bill joined them while his niece stayed with a younger set at a nearby table. Meli saw her dancing with Case once. Bill asked Meli to dance. Tor, engaged in conversation with Milt, smiled with benign consent, which made her fume.

As the evening slipped away on silver wings, Meli was asked by more of the younger men to dance. Of these, she liked Case the best. And, she admitted, she liked Bill better than any of the men she had thus far met, including Case.

She found the wealthy professor to be a thoughtful person and one who listened with real interest to another's opinion. If he disagreed, he said so, but without making her feel defensive. As they danced, they fought a lengthy verbal duel over the benefits of technology. The isolation of Meli's mountain retreat encouraged voracious reading during the long evenings and she had a good memory for facts, which she ably used to support her arguments. The debate raged good-naturedly between them until both ran out of steam.

They lapsed into a companionable silence and Meli half closed her eyes and hummed softly to the beautiful music of a Strauss waltz. She felt herself encircled in an intimate embrace, drawn nearer until her cheek naturally settled on Bill's shoulder. It was comforting and not at all like Tor's demanding embrace.

A funny sensation at the back of her neck brought her head up. She looked around. Tor was dancing with a woman whose name Meli didn't remember. Over the woman's head he gave her a slightly cynical grin, then moved on around the floor.

He was behaving well. Meli was grateful for that.

But then, she should have known he wouldn't really do anything to embarrass her in front of his friends. In a way, it was flattering to have him so determined to win her back to their affair, but she was equally set on love and marriage. He had affection for her, but not the love she needed. And he was completely against marriage.

In view of his past knowledge of matrimony, she couldn't blame him for that. But his attitude was not her problem, and she wasn't going to concern herself with trying to change it. She became aware of Bill's voice and forced her attention to a funny tale about college life and its trials and tribulations.

Before the evening ended, Bill asked to take her for a ride the next afternoon. They would stop and have an early supper before he brought her home. However, Tor had already made plans that took up most of Meli's free time. And when she was free, Bill wasn't.

"I'll call you later in the week, then," Bill promised.

"Yes, that would be lovely," Meli said, encouraging him.

Several minutes were spent in saying good night to the rest of the revelers before Paula, Tor and Meli left the ball. They were invited to attend a champagne breakfast at more than one home.

"Just what we need," Paula sighed when they were finally on their way, "more champagne. And with eggs, no less!"

* * *

The second week of her visit passed in the same flurry of activity as the first. During the day, Meli posed for Paula wearing the white dress silk-screened with flowers. She sat in a dreamy trance on the low rock wall at the end of a patio. Behind her, the pink flowers formed a line of color against the woods.

Bill called twice that week, catching her between his classes. Her initial liking of him continued to increase. He was a mature, considerate person. Just the type a woman could grow to love in time.

On Saturday, Tor escorted her and Paula to another party, this time at Milt and Andy's home, which was not as large as Tor's but was crowded with furniture. Andy was an antique collector. She took Meli on a tour of the house. By the time they returned to the gathering party, Meli and her hostess were fast friends.

Meli was disappointed that Bill wasn't present. She had expected him.

Tor was attentive to her needs, seeing that she wasn't left alone, but he didn't hover over her. She met and talked with several men, all of whom worked for SCL, Milt told her.

"And all of them single," he added, bringing a blush to her cheeks. For a minute she feared that Tor had let Milt and Andy in on the secret of her quest, but she saw that Milt was teasing her. He called a tall, attractive man over, made some jokes about doing his bit for the singles, and left them.

They chatted amicably for several minutes, covering the usual topics of their homes and jobs. Meli looked around a couple of times, wondering where Tor was. It was getting late and she was tired. It had been a hectic week.

"Meli."

Relieved, Meli spun to face her escort and encountered thin air. Her eyes darted in a half circle about them. She was positive Tor had said her name. Somewhat baffled, she smiled at a quip from the manager of a design group in an electronics division of SCL. A sudden anxious impatience invaded her.

Across the room, the doors were open. A movement in the shadows just beyond them held her attention, and then Tor stepped forward. She was instantly mesmerized by his compelling, unsmiling scrutiny.

"Excuse me," she murmured, and glided across the dim room where other couples were swaying to soft music.

Tor met her, his arms opening to receive her trembling body and hold her close as if comforting her. They moved in time to an old ballad, their lips silent, their eyes speaking.

A rush of emotion so strong it couldn't be denied had overwhelmed her when her eyes had met his. An unfathomable sadness pulsed through her heart, then flowed outward through her veins until her entire being was caught in it.

She wanted to weep and cry out with the pain of this silent anguish that she didn't understand. Only the most primitive regions of her soul could comprehend it, it was so primal. A small gasp was torn from her aching throat.

Tor pressed her head to his chest, and gradually the strong, steady beat of his heart calmed her. When the music stopped, she simply stood there, waiting.

"Are you ready to go?" he asked in his quiet tones that could soothe and excite simultaneously.

"Yes, please." She sounded exhausted, and he hurried to call Paula and get them home.

"Are you okay?" the older woman asked, looking at Meli's pale face when they stood in the entrance of Tor's house.

"She's tired," Tor answered. "Come on, off to bed with you." He spoke with deliberate cheer and guided her down the hall to her room. At the door, he turned her with a gentle touch of his hands on her shoulders. "Meli."

She lifted her lashes to stare at him with a haunted gaze.

"Do you want to stay with me tonight?" he asked softly.

Her voice was a whisper of leaves on the night wind. "I don't know," she confessed.

His hands dropped to his sides and clenched into fists. "Tell me how to help you."

She closed her eyes. "Leave me alone. Please. Let me go." She didn't know what she was asking. There was only this feeling of being trapped and in pain. Tor was the source.

"I can't," he groaned. "You're mine. You're

asking me to throw out a part of my life and I can't. You're telling me I have to forget two years as if they never happened. I won't forget. Not ever."

"You will. Someday you will."

"No," he said fiercely. "And I won't let you forget, either!"

Her voice seemed to come from a long way off and she tried to smile. "I won't need any reminders of my long-distance lover. He was my very best friend."

Fingers capable of choking the life from her settled at the base of her throat. "We'll have more than past memories," he promised. Holding her head in a warm clasp, he lifted her face and kissed her soft lips, once. And then he opened the door and shooed her inside.

She got ready for bed quickly, sliding between the covers and bundling them about her neck as if she were in zero-degree weather. She was cold with the knowledge that she had failed. In spite of her intentions, she had fallen in love with her former lover all over again.

At breakfast the next morning she tried to act normal. Tor gave her a section of the Sunday paper to read, his quick appraisal bringing a forced smile to her face as she took it.

His intention of getting her back in his bed hadn't changed, she knew. Her wavering determination to stay out was in question. Loving him made it much harder. During the long hours of the night she had realized that her love had lain dormant in her heart all this time, like a seed waiting for the warmth of spring to bring it to bud. The southern spring had proven so much warmer than the northern one. Her love was in full bloom.

She gazed at him as he sat across from her. Everything about him seemed golden.

When she was finished eating, he stood suddenly and held out a hand to her. "Come on. Let's take a walk."

Paula's glance was briefly inquiring, but then she returned to the article she was reading. Tor released Meli's hand when they were down the gallery steps and on the lawn. He led her across the green expanse, through the patch of woods, and then along the little stream that gurgled with a happy sound.

Stopping, he leaned against a tree, his eyes going dark as they surveyed her expressionless face. "So where are we now?" he asked, his right brow lifting just a little.

She shrugged. Grasping a tree branch over her head, she held on to it with both hands and let her body lean over the chattering flow of water. As far as she could see, they were where they had been yesterday and the day before.

The humor left his face. "I want an answer! What did last night mean?"

"Nothing."

From the corner of her eye she saw his fist clench in fury with her, but she had spoken only the truth. While she loved him to distraction, that made no difference to their future. Except that she would go back to Montana without a husband or a lover. She was positive on that score.

"So you're still looking for a husband?" he gritted. He moved closer to her arched form and she felt the menace in every line of his body. He wore an old pair of cutoffs and a teeshirt, exposing the ripple of smooth muscle and leaving his long, supple legs bare.

The sadness of the previous evening returned, not as staggering but just as deep. It was all she could do not to throw herself into her lover's arms and take the comfort she knew he would give.

"I could have taken you to my room. You wouldn't have refused," he said almost to himself, as if he were continuing an internal argument.

She bowed her head to this truth. "Why didn't you?"

His faint laugh was self-mocking. "I had to face my own conscience. You were too vulnerable for some reason. I took advantage of that once before." She knew he referred to their first meeting.

"Oh, Tor," she murmured. Why did he have to be so perceptive, so gentle, so understanding of her? How could she help loving a man like that?

"Are you still determined to go ahead with this husband hunt?" he asked in a voice rough with emotion.

It would be a long time before she could contemplate another in his place. She would return to her home and break off the association with him entirely. Someday she might meet a man to love as she loved this one, but she didn't truly believe that.

"Are you?" he demanded.

Staunchly, she nodded, unable to speak past the knot of tears in her throat.

His face hardened like the wall of granite at Stone Mountain. "Then my warning stands. I'll do everything I can to prevent it . . . except physically seduce you." His eyes swept down her jeans and shirt, undressing her in the process, laying bare her silken skin with his memories of her. "Although I do that every time I look at you."

Meli pushed against the branch, swung back, and pivoted to walk several feet from him before facing that raw masculine desire again. She was shaken by the intensity of his need and by the matching response it called to life in her. The fire blazed, threatening to dissolve her resolutions. Her hands ached to touch him, to slip over the surfaces of his body that she knew as well as her own. "Don't," she pleaded with him and herself.

"Yes," he said inexorably. "I'm going to remind you in a hundred ways of what we have . . . in a look . . . a word," he promised softly. "You're a stubborn female, but I'm an implacable male." He laughed as her mouth tightened mutinously. "And you can't see what's right under your nose," he concluded.

"I can see where this discussion is leading. Nowhere! You have no claims on me, Tor Halliday. I am not going to continue in an affair with you and that's final!" She put her hands on her hips and glared at his confident grin.

"Oh, is that right?" he inquired, stalking nearer.

"Yes! So there's no use in your beating a dead horse," she finished in a breathless fury, disturbed by the way he was looking at her. He was once more amused, she saw by the lift of his dark brows. Her own contracted as she prepared to argue some more, but a sound caught her attention.

She and Tor glanced around at the same time. From across the fence and behind a group of thin saplings a horse and rider gazed at the quarreling couple. Their voices would have easily carried the distance to her. With a nod, Mary Beth turned her mount and rode away over the little hillock that hid her house from view.

"Oh, no!" Meli exclaimed as she recognized the disaster written in the other woman's smile. "I'm going home to Montana."

A long arm snaked out and grabbed hers. "No, you're not. You are going to stay right here and face this down."

For a long minute they glared at each other; then she made a disrespectful face at him. "They're your friends and neighbors. You'll be the one who has to deal with the gossip."

"Then let me worry about it."

His other hand curved around the back of her neck, his thumb tracing a fiery path under her jawline. "Would you take offense if I were to kiss you one time?" His eyes narrowed as he studied her face for an answer. Slowly he drew her forward to his waiting lips.

She took the one step needed to bring her close enough. Her hands lifted to rest on his chest and his heat penetrated her palms. Reluctantly she raised her face, unable to stop the action.

He claimed the prize, taking her mouth by storm, parting her lips, plundering the moist cavity inside like a man starving.

"Babe, babe," he whispered much later. "It's been so long. Night after night I've lain in bed, longing to come get you. Do you have any idea?"

"Yes," she said. "Yes, but we can't."

His large hands caressed her back, pushing under her shirt to touch her skin. "I know." His anguished statement pierced her last reserve and she clung to him, drawing a gasp as her body arched to his. He moved his hands to her buttocks, gripping them with gentle urgency, lifting her to him, driving them both to the brink of surrender.

"Oh, love, I can't stand . . ." The hunger was too much. She had to have him. Completely. All of him. Her fingers searched over his body as he bent over her.

He carried her into the privacy of the woods, finding a spot to lay her down and then joining her on the thick bed of fallen leaves. Unbuttoning her shirt, he quickly found what he desired. His tongue circled her taut nipple until she was gasping, and then he took it into his mouth and sucked his fill of the sweetness he found there.

"You are a honeypot," he told her, his voice a panting rasp as he moved up to her ear and his hand took the place of his mouth on her breast.

She squirmed against him, demanding more from him with every writhing movement. She was a silken flame dancing over his flesh with her light, caressing touches. He groaned deep in his chest as both her hands slid into the waistband of his cutoffs.

Their mouths met, merged into an endless joining of moist lips and searching tongues. Their bodies shaped themselves together with ingrained knowledge of each curve and plane. Legs opened and pressed intimately against the barrier of clothing for the final contact.

With his seeking lips, he found the pulse beating out of control at the base of her throat. Then his mouth moved on, sliding along her skin with a moist, sucking motion that shot wild sensations down into her chest.

Her fingers clenched desperately in the muscles of his back. "Now," she whimpered. "Now, please, my love."

"Shhhh." He silenced her plea with fingers rubbing her passion-swollen lips. He moved his hands into the tousled layers of her hair and held her ready for his kiss. He nibbled with seductive little bites on her lower lip, then gave the same attention to her upper one. "My God, but you're beautiful!" His eyes swept hotly over her straining figure as she lay supine beneath him, nestled in the bed of leaves.

Flames licked over her; she yearned for his complete touch and the release she knew that he could give her. Mindlessly, she sought the sweet oblivion of ecstasy with no thought of withholding herself from her lover's masterful touch.

His hand caught both of hers, held them above her head in one strong clasp. His free hand then slowly meandered along the damp contours of her ribs, flowed over her small breasts.

"I want you, babe. It's killing me not to strip these clothes out of the way and take what's mine . . . and yours." He offered himself in exchange, freely admitting he would surrender himself to her passion as she did to his. "But I won't." With great tenderness, he kissed her exposed, contracted nipple, savoring the flavor of the tiny bud.

"Why?" The word was spoken in a low tone.

"I gave my word," he said. "You can hold your own in a verbal skirmish with me, but this, this is stronger than both of us. I won't take physical advantage of you." A smile flickered through his eyes. "I know your passionate nature."

Slowly she regained control. "Then why start something that you knew you weren't going to finish."

His grin was sardonic. "Well, I didn't know for sure that I could keep from going all the way." His finger traced the blush along her cheek. "I only meant to remind you of what we had on that level. I was afraid you might be forgetting that while you were thinking of other men."

Her laughter mimicked the quiet burble of the brook behind them. "Tell me how to forget!" she invited. "That's the problem."

He drew her to her feet, fastened her shirt for her with capable motions, and smoothed his own clothing. "I'm not going to let you forget even one spark of desire, not for a moment." His eyes narrowed as he looked her over to see if she was presentable. He combed the leaves out of her hair with his fingers.

"So, the battle is rejoined, right?" She cocked her head at a saucy angle to look up at his towering height.

He kissed her nose, ran his hands over her breasts, down over the flare of her hips, intimately along her thighs, back along the center of her body up to her neck.

"I wish I weren't such an honorable type, bound by my word," he complained soulfully. "I'll probably be swimming from midnight to dawn tonight." He led the way through the woods. "And you'll be sleeping like a baby, blast it!"

Meli followed along meekly at his heels. He had a strange sense of honor, she thought. It was all right for him to try to win her with words, to taunt her with her desire, to seduce her with his eyes . . . just as long as he kept his hands off her while he did! Lordy, she might have to join in the swimming marathon.

Paula caught her when they returned to the house. Dressed once more in the gypsy outfit, Meli sat for hours in various poses while the artist sketched busily and Tor looked on with great interest. Later in the afternoon, friends dropped over and they held an impromptu swimming party. As day ambled into evening, Tor cooked steaks on the grill and James miraculously served up salad, baked potatoes, corn on the cob, and a superb banana pudding for dessert.

When the stars came out, Paula was prevailed upon to play for them. To Meli's surprise, the woman brought out a guitar and strummed lovely old songs that they could sing to.

Tor wrapped Meli in his terrycloth robe as the night chilled, and he sat at her feet, leaning on her knees while he sang along with her.

The sorrow of the previous night returned but was softer, rounded at the edges into an abiding melancholy that was somehow reassuring. It was as if the pain attested to the reality of her love and the heartbreak that was sure to come when she left. It hurt, but it was better than not loving at all.

For the next three days Tor resumed his indulgent-father act with her. He took her to his office on Monday and introduced her to Betty, his secretary, who was nice, middle-aged, and happily married with two grown children. After introducing her to several single men who worked for him in the huge building, he had lunch brought to his office where he thoroughly discussed all her marriage prospects with a serious face and a wicked gleam in his eyes.

"You didn't like Johnny?" he teased.

The one they were discussing was a cigar-chewing, overweight Lothario who had been struck with instant desire for her, if his leer was anything to go by. Meli cut a piece of prime rib, plopped it into her mouth, and considered the candidate.

"I didn't like his tie," she said.

"Picky," Tor muttered, slathering butter on a yeast roll.

"I think Bill Jordache is the likeliest one of the bunch."

That changed his sunny mood to a thundercloud. "You'd have his niece to contend with. He's her favorite uncle and spoils her rotten."

"Maybe I can root her out of his favor," Meli replied with more confidence and determination than she felt.

"And maybe you would wind up hurt!" he rejoined, clearly out of humor with her now. He refilled her wineglass, making a task of it, then changed the subject when the conversation resumed.

On Wednesday the three of them went to a dinner-dance at the country club. It was in Livingston's honor, sponsored by the Council of the Arts. Meli wore the white skirt and floral top ensemble for the first time. She liked the way the pleated skirt fluttered around her knees, showing off a length of smooth tanned leg.

By now she was quite at home with many of the people she saw there. Milt and Andy were two of those; Case, charmingly lecherous, was another. Bill wasn't present, but he had called her earlier that day and invited her out for a boat ride on Saturday afternoon. She had accepted in spite of Tor's frowning displeasure.

"Light o' me life, would you do the honor of one wee foxtrot or a jig or two?" Case's familiar cadences fell on Meli's ears as soon as the music started.

Gaily, she got up and tripped off to the floor with him under Tor's benevolent gaze.

"You're looking well," she said as they wove their way amid the dancing crowd.

Case released her hand to pull his forelock in a feudal gesture of thanks. "Thank'ee, miss." His humbleness lasted for about two seconds, then he laughed. "And what have you been doing?" he asked.

"Running to parties every night, posing for Paula every day. What a hectic life you Southerners lead!"

He glanced around as if to make sure no one could overhear. "Honey," he said in a low drawl, "you ain't seen half of it yet."

Meli thoroughly enjoyed the young man. He was twenty-eight years old to her twenty-nine, and seemed somehow both older and younger. He was more experienced, but younger at heart than herself, she decided.

Before Case could return her to her group, Livingston caught up with them and took her to the dance floor. He galloped her around as if they were spinning tops out of control. Meli gave up on gay repartee and just tried to hang on. She was out of breath and laughing by the time the music stopped. Another young man cut in when the next tune began, and she was spirited away from the taciturn, intense artist.

Halfway through the number, a hand tapped on her partner's shoulder and Tor smoothly removed her from his embrace. He glided off with her, holding her snugly to himself.

"Are you having a good time?" he asked, looking at her flushed cheeks and sparkling eyes. Tonight she was wearing earrings of rose quartz that he had loaned her from his mother's collection; the gems paled beside her glowing complexion.

"Yes. Don't I always?" She tossed her head in an open challenge. The couple next to them swirled, and Meli saw that the other girl was Mary Beth. Some of her glow faded, but she smiled gamely at the arch smirk on the other's face.

"Yes," he murmured for her ears only. "You're only grouchy when you get less than your eight hours of beauty rest. I wonder if I should mention that to Case or Bill?" he mused with a sober frown on his brow.

She squinted her eyes at him in warning, drawing his quick grin. Catching her to him, he swung her around in circles until she was laughing again.

Later she danced again with Case, then went with him to the refreshment table to pile their plates with treats. While she was selecting items from a tray of fresh vegetables, Case mentioned his mother's garden, telling how the woman loved to putter in it. Then the talk drifted to the terrain around Atlanta.

"You should see the rolling hills of my place with all the pecan trees," he told her.

"I'd love to," she responded warmly.

Case hesitated, visibly unsure about offering the invitation.

"What is it?" she asked.

"Honey, can you take the truth?" A hand on her

arm guided her to one side, out of the way of others who wanted a snack.

"Of course," she said, curious about his secretive manner.

"Well," he drawled, "several of us have wanted to ask you out, but . . . well, there's Tor."

"I don't understand," she said slowly. "Do you mean you felt you would have to invite him, too?"

A slight flush mounted Case's cheeks. "You seem to, ah, belong to him."

Meli's eyes turned to midnight blue. They glittered over the face of her earnest companion and on to the people in the large room. She spied Mary Beth, who was looking at her, but who turned away with a lift of her shoulder.

"Because of what *she's* saying?" Meli nodded toward the other girl.

"Oh, her gossip is generally ignored. She talks about everybody. Actually, it's the signal from a certain person, a flash of blue laser when anyone so much as looks at you . . . or dares to touch you."

Meli stared at him, openmouthed. "You're joking," she gasped.

Case shook his head, the gleam of his usual high spirits back in his eyes. "Tor has Keep Off signs posted all around you. We assumed they were there with your consent. He's always touching you, you know."

"No. No, I don't know," she protested, beginning to get angry as she sought out her underhanded host across the crowded club.

"Yes," Case continued, grinning at her. "He pats your shoulder or pushes your hair back from your face. When you aren't looking, he keeps an eagle eye on everything you do. If you stay with one person too long, he comes after you. Like now."

Meli glanced up to see the subject of their discussion swooping on them like an enraged mountain cat. She realized she was mixing her metaphors. Eagles swoop; cougars stalk. Tor could do both at the same time, she saw as he closed the distance between them and pounced on her.

"I have someone I'd like you to meet," he said suavely, moving her away from Case, who gave a diabolical chuckle at Meli's look of chagrin. "You'll excuse us, old man?" he politely asked the young man, who nodded.

As they moved off, she pulled from the talonlike grasp on her wrist. "You . . . you *cheat*!" she flung at her former lover.

Chapter Eleven

*W*ould you care to repeat that?" he asked politely, the ominous roll of thunder in his voice.

Meli smiled at a passing couple. "You heard me," she said in low tones, maintaining a facade of friendliness.

"I think it's time to go." He cast her a sideways glance that took in the rigidity of her smile.

"I agree!"

By the time they located Paula and ascertained that she wanted to leave with them, and they stopped to speak to several friends who protested their departure, another hour had swept across the face of the clock. With difficulty, Meli retained her poise on the ride home with the chattering Paula and gruffly silent Tor. An unspoken agreement between the warring duo kept up the pretense of peace until they were alone in the library after Paula had gone to her room.

"Now what bee do you have in your bonnet?" Tor quipped, pouring soda into a glass for himself after a refusal of anything by his angry houseguest.

"Don't you dare patronize me, Tor Halliday. Not after what you've done to me . . . you and that infantile femme fatale!"

He cocked one arrogant brow. "That could only be Mary Beth," he surmised. "Nice to have a conspirator in whatever crime it is that I've committed."

"You know what you've done!" She strode with leashed emotion around the room, her eyes flashing dangerously from object to object as if choosing her weapons.

"What?" he asked softly, suddenly out of patience with her dramatic anger.

"Ruined my chances, that's what. Everybody in Georgia thinks I'm your mistress, thanks to you and that . . . that brat!" She flung herself into a chair, pressing a hand to her heated forehead. "You told me this was a crazy idea. I should have listened. I must have been insane to ask a lover to help me find a husband. Naturally, you would sabotage such a plan. Men always have to be the ones to end an affair. Their fragile egos can't handle it when the woman makes the break."

"Now, honey, calm down," he advised.

"I am calm," she said flatly. "So calm I could

scream! Case told me what you were doing. What makes me so mad is the fact that I trusted you!"

A flush spread slowly up his neck and over the hard ridge of jawbone. "Is it my honor that's in question?"

"Honor," she said in disgust. "You wouldn't recognize honor if it were packaged and mailed to you."

Tor stalked over to her and stopped directly in front of her chair. "Watch what you say, Meli. I'll take a lot from you, but there are limits, even for lovers," he warned.

"And I've reached my limit! I'll never believe anything you say again! I was so naive. Until Case told me—"

Tor interrupted, his gaze narrowed and penetrating. "You'd better explain just exactly what our infamous playboy said. And forget the insults and name-calling!"

Turning from her accusing glare, he dropped into a chair and stretched his long legs out in front, crossing them at the ankles. He looked like a lounging cat, but Meli wasn't fooled by his relaxed pose. She recognized the danger signs in the tenseness of his shoulders and the set of his mouth.

Finally she answered, "Case said that when I was with someone else, you look at me."

A sardonic grin greeted that statement. She realized how inane it sounded. "I'm not allowed to look at you?" he inquired.

"It's the way you look. As if you own me."

"I do."

Her eyes flew open at this. "That's not true! You—"

"But it is." He was completely sure of himself. "You belong to me. I told you that."

She decided against arguing in the abstract and went to the next point, her lips thin with anger. "You gave your word that you would keep your hands off me. Case said you were always touching me as if posting No Trespassing signs around my body."

"According to Case."

"Yes. He said that he and his friends had talked about it. Some of them would have liked to invite me out but were put off by the laser glares they received from you."

Tor waved a hand in the air. "There, you see," he said as if arriving at some truth.

"What?" she demanded.

"None of them proved himself potential husband material. What real man would have been put off by a scowl or two?" He took a drink, obviously pleased with his observation.

Meli scowled as he made this point. Then, "There's Mary Beth. I'm sure she's told everyone what she heard in the woods the other day."

His lazy, sexy gaze roamed over her trim figure. "Well," he drawled, "she's telling the truth if she's saying we're lovers."

"We're not!"

"We could be," he reminded her softly.

Clenching her fists in her lap, she tried to keep up a cool front. "Between the two of you, I think you've finished my reputation in this town." Her lips trembled, but when she saw the softening of his expression at her distress she cast him a defiant look.

He leaned forward, resting his forearms on his thighs. "None of those men is worthy of you if he believes malicious gossip from a known trouble-maker."

The anger that had sustained her so far was seeping away. She wanted to throw herself in his arms and seek his comfort, to take his caresses and let herself be soothed. But that would be playing right into his hands.

With a slight toss of her head, she denied herself that easy way out. "There's one person who isn't put off by your sneaky tactics. I have a date with Bill Jordache to go boating on Saturday afternoon and I'm going! I'm also going to accept any other dates he asks for, so don't make any plans for me this next week," she finished triumphantly.

Tor's face went as dark as a storm cloud. His jaw clenched and unclenched. It was awesome to watch the controlling of that fury, and Meli was afraid.

"I'll move to a hotel," she began hesitantly.

He sprang out of the chair in one leaping attack. "No, damn it, you won't. You'll stay right here," he said in a low growl. "And you won't have to worry about my straying hands or proprietary glances. I'm going to New York."

Meli experienced a twang of disappointment. Furiously she forced it down. "Good! How long will you be gone?"

He looked as if he could barely restrain himself

from hitting her. "I leave tomorrow on a ten-day trip." His glance at her was a thunderbolt striking her heart. "I had planned to take you along. My secretary got tickets to several shows."

He tossed this information at her, not as a lure to change her mind, but to let her know what she was going to miss.

Raising her chin, she assumed a disinterested mien, but inside she was swamped with regret. What fun to attend Broadway shows with him! "Then I can get on with my quest," she asserted.

There was no quest, but she wouldn't give him the satisfaction of knowing he had been right. She would date Bill, pretend to consider him, decide against it, and then go home next weekend with a nicely spoken word of thanks to her host and a gift to Paula for her kindness.

Tor walked over to the window and stood with his back to her. "Yes, you can continue your quest," he finally said in quiet tones that contrasted vividly with his fury of a minute ago. He let himself out the side door and left the room without saying good night.

He was gone the next morning when Meli joined Paula in the gallery for breakfast. The older woman watched her push food around on her plate but said nothing about Tor's absence or her lack of appetite. Instead, she made several plans for the next two days and rushed Meli through them without giving her time for brooding.

On Saturday, Meli went on the boat ride and

accepted a date for dinner that night. Bill was a relaxing person who put no demands or pressure on her that she couldn't handle. He kissed her good night when he brought her home, but that was all. They went out six nights of the ten that Tor was gone.

On the day Tor was due back, Paula went out to dinner with friends and Meli went to a movie with Bill. She was nervous during the show and didn't remember much of it when it was over. Bill drove her straight back to the house.

"May I come in?" he asked at the door.

"Of course," she said as she opened the door. "I'll get us some coffee." Meli led the way into the living room. The curtains at the open windows were lightly stirred by the pleasant air that flowed through the house. The sleeves of her boldly printed full-sleeved blouse fluttered against her shapely arms. Her cinnamon slacks hugged the curve of her hips.

James brought the coffee on a tray, then left. Meli served the aromatic brew herself. Leaning comfortably into the nook of the sofa, she smiled sleepily at Bill, who sat next to her.

"I've had a very pleasant time this past week with you," he told her with deep feeling in his voice.

Alarmed by the intimate note, she straightened up. "So have I," she replied truthfully, but cautiously.

"I'd like to continue it into the future," he said huskily, "a long and happy future." His eyes were warm with hope.

Her breath caught. Was he proposing? Now that the very thing she had said she wanted was coming about, her only reaction was one of distress. How could she stop him? Could she tactfully head him off in order to avoid an outright refusal? Why hadn't she seen this coming?

There had been no passion, no deep personal discussions between them during the past week, she reminded herself. While Bill had let her see that he enjoyed her company, he had certainly never hinted that his feelings went much deeper. She felt terrible about it. Had she misled him?

"I have to leave soon," she said.

She was waiting for a call from the airline about her reservation. It was no secret. Bill knew she was going home sometime during the next week.

"I know. That's what I wanted to talk to you about." He paused, a touch of uncertainty in his manner, while she searched for something, anything, to say to stop him. "I'm not prying, but am I correct in assuming that whatever was between you and Tor is over?" His gray eyes regarded her intently.

She sensed the importance of his question. "Yes," she said, "that's correct, but . . ."

"Then may I come to visit you at your home?" he asked.

For a moment she was speechless and numb. His meaning wasn't at all clear. "Are you asking to . . . to take his place?" The question was slow in coming. Her thoughts seemed all in a tangle.

His quick smile was one of pleasure. "Yes." He

reached for and took both her hands in his. Bringing them to his lips, he kissed along each knuckle as if he were sealing a pact with her. Meli could only stare stupidly at him.

So much for her worries about not hurting his feelings when he asked her to marry him, she thought in semihysteria. He only wanted to be her lover! Another Tor who dropped in out of the blue when he could get time out of his busy schedule. It was funny. Except that she wanted very much to cry.

There was a click; then a harsh, sneering voice inquired, "I take it congratulations are in order?" Tor stood inside the door leading out onto the patio. His smile was hateful.

Meli turned her incredulous eyes to his black scrutiny. A smile broke over her face and she pressed her quickly released hands over her lips, holding back the laughter his appearance was summoning forth. This whole thing was so crazy!

"When's the big date?" he mocked.

"Date?" Bill echoed.

Meli giggled. Both men looked at her. "He doesn't want to marry me. He just wants to visit me once in a while like you did."

Tor's gaze swung back to Bill. He looked like an enraged bull. "You bastard!" he said, and leaped for the older man.

Bill stood, then sidestepped and kicked out at the same moment. Tor sank to the carpet and sat there with a comical expression on his face. He lifted a hand to his chin.

"What the hell did you hit me with?" His eyes were slightly dazed.

"My foot," Bill informed him laconically.

Meli flew to Tor, kneeling beside him to examine his bruised jaw. She darted Bill one hard, speaking glance. "Get out of here," she gritted at him, returning his stare with unflinching courage.

Shrugging, he picked up his jacket and ambled out. A few seconds later the front door closed behind him; then they heard his car start and drive off.

"Are you all right?"

"I'm fine. Are you all right?"

She sat back on her heels. Her eyes dropped. "Yes, of course I am. Why shouldn't I be? I wasn't the one who got a karate kick to the chin."

"That wasn't a proposal of marriage I interrupted," he reminded her gently. "I wanted to kill him for insulting you like that!"

Standing and moving aside while he got to his feet, she felt a fire starting to burn out of control. "What did you expect me to receive, a person with my reputation?" she asked bitterly.

He winced from the truth of her statement. "Babe, I'm sorry. I never meant this to happen. I just wanted to prevent you from doing anything foolish."

"You just wanted to keep me for yourself! And the only foolish thing I ever did was allow you in my life in the first place. But that is a mistake that I can rectify."

Meli spun abruptly and ran from the room, along the corridor, and into her bedroom. She grabbed her suitcases and strewed them about the floor, then pulled clothes out of drawers and the closet and folded them as fast as she could.

It wasn't until Tor came in, looked at her, and pulled her into his arms that she knew she was crying. Slow tears ran down her face in a continuous trickle.

"Don't," he pleaded. "Don't cry. It tears me apart."

"You'll get over it," she said with a cynical laugh. "Let me go, Tor. I'm going home, and this time I'm going to stay there. You're not to visit me. You won't be welcome." She stood stiff in his embrace until he released her.

Ignoring him, she returned to her frantic packing. She pushed the clothing Tor had bought her to the end of the closet and removed her long skirt, the pink suit, the plum-colored dress, and her two best pantsuits and put them in her suitbag, then zipped and folded it in preparation for the trip home. She stuffed underwear into the corners of her cases.

He stepped in front of her. "I want you to stay with me, Meli. I'll make all this up to you, I swear. You'll come out with an unblemished record."

Brushing her bangs off her forehead, she hardened herself to the quiet promise of his words and the somber plea of his eyes. "I wouldn't stay within a thousand miles of you. I'm going home where I'm my own person."

"Babe . . ."

"Don't say anything else," she cried. Forcing herself to breathe deeply, she sought control. Walking around him, she resumed her task. "You know, it's true that you don't know a person until you see him on his own turf."

Tor studied her change of mood. "What do you mean?" He absently fingered his sore chin.

Meli was stabbed with remorse that he had been hurt because he had wanted to defend her, but then she reminded herself that he was the main reason she had needed defending. She had learned a couple of things about Bill Jordache tonight, too.

"I never knew how underhanded, conniving, and selfish you were until I came here, so the visit wasn't a complete loss."

"Is that what you think?" he asked softly.

The smile that curled around her mouth was scornful. "Yes, that's exactly what I think!"

He moved nearer. "Then nothing I do will change your mind, will it?"

She closed her two large pieces of luggage and snapped the locks into position. "Nothing," she agreed.

Two large hands settled on her shoulders, turning her to face his wrath. A flicker of fear flashed through her blood, but she wouldn't back down.

"So it won't affect your black opinion of me if I take what I want." His voice was ominous with threat. "A little payment for my hospitality, shall we say?"

"I'll hate you forever," she warned as he backed her toward her bed. The flicker increased to a tremble.

"Go ahead. You won't be around, so it won't bother me."

With a sudden push, he sent her sprawling, his body coming down on hers before she could roll to the side. Looking into his eyes directly above her own, she was intimidated by the cold fury she could read there. He had never looked at her in that manner before. His lips fell on hers in a savage attack that made her go instantly weak, but not in fear. She experienced only a deep, primitive longing.

Moment after breathless moment sped by, marked by the wild beating of her heart. Clutching the white lace of the bedspread, she held her arms rigidly at her side and refused to give in to her clamoring senses as his kiss ground her into submission.

When he released her mouth, it was to ravage the sensitive skin along her neck; she moaned in protest. "Don't. I don't want this."

"Yes, you do," he denied hotly, caught up in his own passionate need to punish her and claim her for himself again. "I've taken all I can. You're driving me insane," he gasped as he bit her ear gently but with urgent hunger.

His hand swept along her side, reached the prize and covered it. Her nipple hardened against his palm. He laughed with male triumph.

"No!" She pushed against his shoulders as his leg

parted her own and pressed intimately with increasing ardor. Tears began to seep from the corners of her eyes, soaking the lace beneath her head.

"Meli." He moaned her name in despair when his lips encountered the wetness. "Oh, God, don't cry! Not now!"

"I don't want you to make love to me," she whispered.

He smoothed the hair from her forehead as gently as a mother with a child. "You've forgotten how it is with us," he murmured.

"I don't want to remember. I only want to know my husband, no one else." Her eyes were tightly closed.

He went absolutely still for a second before flinging himself from her. "All right, go to another man, marry him, have your kids and your companionship! But sometime, when you're in his arms, remember how it was with us and see how much you're missing." He started from the room.

Meli lifted herself from the rumpled covers. "I won't be missing anything! It'll be better!" she shouted at his back.

He slammed out.

Weakly, she pulled herself up against the pillows. A riot of emotions raged through her as she relived the past hour. Men! she thought. She pounded her fists on the bed. She wished she could rid the world of them. What did a woman want with one? Trouble, nothing but trouble and aggravation, that's what they were. Arrogant slobs!

Faintly, from a distance, she heard the slam of

another door. Tor's bedroom, she surmised. He thought he was so great as a lover. She ought to show him!

Her eyes brightened. She *would* show him. Flouncing off the bed, she went into the bath. There she took a shower, then put on a generous splash of perfume and powder. She rummaged through the nightgowns in her suitcase until she found the one she wanted—the midnight blue with the provocative lace inserts.

Revenge firmed the lines of her soft lips as she opened her door and peered down the hall. Paula wasn't back yet; James had gone to his quarters for the night. Like a shimmering shadow, she slipped along the hall and up the stairs.

His bedroom was much larger than hers. The huge bed was custom designed with an elaborate headboard of shelves going to the ceiling. A padded chest, as long as the bed was wide, was positioned at the footboard. A blue satin comforter was turned down to disclose blue striped sheets.

She was halfway across the room when Tor came in from the bath. His hair was damp and a towel was tucked around his lean hips.

"What are you doing in here?" he growled, remnants of his anger visible in the lines around his mouth.

She was bold in her answer. "I came to finish what you started . . . what you've started twice." She advanced on him. Her smile was pure female anticipation.

"Why?" His perusal took in her appearance from

her head to her toes, then came back to her eyes to seek clues there for this about-face.

"You'll see." She reached for the towel. "Get in bed," she ordered in faintly mocking tones. "I'm going to make love to you."

"What about the promise not to seduce you?" A note of perplexity crept into the question. His face grew stern. "The other day my sense of honor saved you; tonight your tears did. If you stay in here much longer, nothing will."

"Thank you for the warning," she quipped lightly, "but you aren't the one doing the seducing. I am. And I made no promises, remember? I don't have to keep my hands off you."

Her smile was brilliant with promise as, with a sudden movement, she flicked the cloth from around his waist.

His hands reached for her, but she stepped out of reach.

"Ahh," she drawled, taking in his powerful, masculine physique. "Very nice." She laughed, satisfied with her maneuvers as she watched his body respond.

Tor placed his hands on his hips and planted his feet in an open stance that made no attempt to hide anything from her sight—which would have been impossible anyway. His smile matched hers. "What now?" he asked, beginning to enjoy this new game.

Flicking her head to the side, she pointed to the bed. "In there."

Obligingly, he walked over to the massive structure, threw the comforter back until it rested on the long chest. Then he lay down on the striped sheets, hands propped behind his head, a grin of expectation on his face.

She slowly unfastened the tie of the blue robe, letting it slip off her shoulders to the floor. Moving to the bed, she stood there letting the tension build to tantalizing proportions while she watched his eyes darkening. His hard body was ready for hers.

When she lifted the hem of her gown out of the way and moved one knee onto the bed, his arms came out, reaching for her. She stopped.

"Put your hands behind your head or on the headboard and keep them there," she commanded.

His eyes rounded with surprise, but when she didn't budge, he reluctantly moved his hands back over his head. "I'm ready," he said.

"I'll be the judge of that," she announced coolly. "This is my game; I'll call the shots." She wanted no doubt in his mind about who was in charge.

A frown creased the smooth plane of his brow. He wasn't all that sure he liked this new order of things. She chuckled as she accurately read his expression.

"Relax, love. I'll see that you enjoy it," she reassured him. The lift of her brow was sardonic as she took her pleasure at his expense.

"Tell me why I'm getting this strange feeling of being used for some kind of revenge," he asked as she studied his body like a painter beginning a new canvas.

She had forgotten his incredible perception where

she was concerned. Not that it mattered if he knew what was happening; she was still determined to carry through.

"You're getting vibes." With this enigmatic answer trembling between them, she raised her other leg to the bed and sank to her knees beside him so that his entire body was within her reach.

Placing both hands in the middle of his chest, she began a slow, lingering journey down to his ankles, her pressing fingers massaging little channels of delight that brought forth a gasp from him as she separated her hands to follow the lines of his steel-corded thighs.

The hair-silkened skin of his legs was warm beneath her palms. Bending down, she nibbled on his toes, raising her lashes to glance up the length of his body and meet the unblinking stare he turned on her.

His hands caught under the edge of the headboard to hold his slipping control in place.

Sweeping back up his legs, she paused to let her fingers play in the curling thatch of body hair. The muscles stood out on his biceps.

Laughing, she swooped with a graceful plunge until her mouth rested on his chest. She teased his tiny nipple into a pebbly response, then did the same with the other. Her hands rubbed ceaselessly along his sides.

A stroking sensation along her back warned her in time. She lunged off the bed. "Do you want me to leave?" she demanded.

"No," he swore passionately.

"Then get your hands back up there."

She didn't move until he had done as she had ordered. Then she climbed back up on the bed. Her own blood began to surge at the evidence of his desire. Her orders for obedience didn't extend to his eyes, and in every nerve she was aware of his continuous perusal, which was getting more and more heated.

"This is fantastically exciting," he told her softly, evidently deciding to add the seduction of his voice to that of his gaze.

"Yes, it is." She smiled beatifically at him.

Suspicion appeared in his eyes. "You aren't planning on going so far then stopping, are you? If you are . . ." His voice went low with implied menace.

She shook her head. "Oh, no. This is going all the way. But at my pace."

He settled himself more comfortably in the sheets. "Help yourself." His grin was confident once more. "I'll probably be out of my mind before this is over, but what the hell!"

"Exactly," she agreed, with soft laughter ruffling the word.

He cooperated with her. Holding nothing back, he let her see what pleased him the most. For herself, she found that his half-murmured encouragements sparked an answer from her.

Once more kneeling beside him, she used her mouth to carry the feverish message of her revenge. By the movements of his body, she knew it was getting increasingly difficult for him to control the hot pulse of need that was in him.

The muscles of his thighs contracted violently when her lips touched him in intimate caresses designed to bring him to the brink of ecstasy as he had done with her so many times. But she wouldn't permit him to release his hold on the bed.

"Witch," he gasped, his voice hoarse with longing.

"Isn't this good?" she taunted him.

"Yes," he whispered. "Yes, it's good." And when she glanced into his eyes, all the teasing mood left her and she found she was far from thoughts of revenge. The meeting of the eyes was a meeting of the souls. Meli was filled with a basic drive to please him—this man who had captured her heart and imagination from the moment they had met—and in pleasing him, to please herself. It was one and the same thing.

The needs of her heart and her body melded into one vast burning desire. He was Tor, her lover, her friend. And she wanted this time to be special above all others.

Exploring with greater thoroughness, she found every tiny erotic nerve ending that he possessed. His splendid oak-hard body moved sensuously under her touch. The tension in her own body became unbearable.

Lying beside him, her eyes never leaving him, she allowed herself to roll against his length. She placed her leg over his, and she gasped as he immediately caught the limb between his, holding her thigh pressed tightly between his own. Twisting slightly, he pushed his advantage by moving his leg into the space between hers that was created for his blatant, masculine frame.

He executed a series of slow movements calculated to drive her wild. As he felt her response, he moved, his leg locking over her hips with a sudden lunge that drove the breath from her gasping body.

"Come to me," he invited in a husky plea.

Swinging her body over his, she accepted him into the circle of her womanhood, lowering herself slowly until her breasts brushed the golden hairs of his chest. Moving back and forth, she tortured both of them until they were aching with sensation.

"Let me touch you, babe," he pleaded. "Take off your gown."

"No, not yet." Desperately, she held on to her sanity. If he touched her, he would take charge, and that she didn't want. This was still her game, although the play had gone out of it long ago, as had the revenge. Now she only wanted to love him and bring him joy through her touch.

Rational thought was washed away in a flood of yearning. She sat up, raised her gown over her head, and tossed it off the bed.

His chest lifted in a gasping groan of anticipation. As she leaned over him, he brought his head up until his mouth could reach her taut nipples. With his tongue, he traced fiery circles, wringing a sighing moan from her. He moved from one to the other.

Her hand slipped behind him to hold his head in place.

When she could stand it no longer, she slid back from his moist embrace. Her body moved on his, slowly at first, then faster as it found the rhythm of mutual excitement.

The impassioned arousal spread upward through her, forced her breath in and out of her lungs as their bodies worked in unison to find the ultimate release.

"Tor," she cried. "Oh, love."

His raised knees helped control the depth of her lovemaking as the firm mounds of her buttocks slipped with fluid abrasion against his thighs. She fought for control, not wanting it to end just yet.

"Please, love, let me help you," Tor urgently demanded, his face contorted with his own effort to hold himself back.

"Yes!"

At once, hands closed around her hips as her lover matched his movement to hers, not taking charge but riding the crest with her, holding her safely in his embrace until they had ridden out the wild, crashing storm to its climax.

She sank onto his chest, where he held her until their breaths slowed and became inaudible. His hands caressed her back and she could feel his lips on her hair.

The heart pounding under her ear gradually slowed, and Meli rolled from his arms, exhausted and saddened. Getting up, she found her gown and robe, put them on, and moved toward the door.

"Meli, stay," he said.

She shook her head, a sense of finality in her movements. It was finished now, she thought. There was nothing more to say . . . except goodbye, and this she had said in her heart. Her lovemaking had been her last goodbye.

Chapter Twelve

*Y*ou could come to my place," Paula said again. They were at the airport now.

Meli shook her head. "I need to go home, to touch base with myself, I think. Don't forget your promise to come visit me in August."

"I won't forget. There's your boarding call," Paula said, listening to the announcement. "I wish you were staying . . ."

"Meli, stay." The voice from last night spoke in her mind. She thought she would hear it forever— the voice of the rejected lover who can't comprehend defeat.

But at breakfast, when she had informed them she had gotten a reservation on that morning's flight to Montana, he had merely nodded, his eyes disclosing nothing of what he was feeling. He had asked Paula to drive her down to the airport.

"I thought you and Tor might get married," Paula said, a frown of disappointment marring her smooth face. "You're so *right* for each other. Didn't you ever talk about it?"

"Actually, we have discussed the subject a number of times," Meli admitted. She permitted herself one tight smile.

"And?"

"We agreed to disagree," Meli said enigmatically. She made sure she had her boarding pass, leaned over to kiss her hostess on the cheek, and said her final farewell. She would miss Paula, who was the closest thing to a sister she had ever had.

Meli settled in her seat; the plane took off, droned its way across the United States, and arrived at its destination without mishap. She caught the shuttle to Kalispell, where Fletch and Greta picked her up in the truck.

The motherly woman was obviously dying to know all about the visit, so Meli supplied several anecdotes as they slowly wended their way to the camp over the rough gravel road. She described every party she had been to, told them about Livingston, rhapsodized about the lovely country around Atlanta.

"And when will Tor be returning?" Fletch asked, as if Tor lived in Montana instead of in Georgia.

She answered easily, without a break, for she had been expecting the question. "I'm not sure. You know how his schedule is." She shrugged, smiling, and told them about Case, the lecherous playboy who had become her friend.

They were still chuckling when they reached the camp. Meli refused Greta's offer of supper. She picked up a few items from the store and went to her own cabin, glad to be alone at last.

When Fletch left after helping her with her luggage, she built a fire to drive out the damp and the chill of disuse that seemed to accumulate in an empty building.

She removed some dough from the freezer and set it in a loaf pan on the hearth to rise. As the last rays of late May sun haloed the western mountain peaks, she removed her travel clothing, put on her flannel nightgown and quilted booties, and began the task of unpacking her suitcases.

It seemed to take a long time. Each item of clothing invoked a poignant memory of time spent with Tor. Tor laughing, Tor playing, Tor teasing her. Tor kissing her.

Tor angry with her, sarcastic about her husband quest; Tor feeling sorry for her, worrying about her when she was hurt. Tor, her lover and best friend.

Hanging the long black skirt in the back of the walk-in closet, she wondered if she would ever wear it again—or any of the clothes she had bought for the trip. Probably she would. Her family had never been wealthy enough to throw out good stuff just because it brought painful memories.

And memories fade. She had told Tor he would forget. He would. Oh, not entirely, but someday their association would bring only a nostalgic shine to the eye. That was the way she wanted it. Wasn't it? she questioned, as a pang of sadness pierced her. Well, it was the way it had to be.

If she had harbored some hope that he would suddenly realize he loved her madly, it had been effectively buried under his wall of silence that morning. He hadn't even said goodbye, just a "So long, babe," and he took off to his room to get ready for work.

Later, with her fleece robe belted tightly around her, she went outside and sat on the step of her small porch, watching the shadows deepen in the woods and listening to the murmuring of the awakening trees.

Soon this solid tranquility would disappear with the influx of humanity into the area. There would be the pleasant smell of several campfires in the air and the high piping of children's voices playing hide-and-seek among the sibilant forest sentinels.

Strangers would meet and exchange greetings and ask after each other's home places and future vacation plans:

"Where are you going from here?"

"Thought we'd take in Yellowstone."

"We just came from there. Fantastic place. Wait till you see the geysers!"

The summer was a time of friendliness. Then the autumn would come. People would drive through the mountains to watch the display of color as leaves died a russet and golden death.

With winter's snow, a younger crowd would show

up, although more and more families were enjoying that season's sports too. There would be skiing and tramping through the snow during the day and singing around the fireplace in the lounge at night.

Last winter she had joined in the festivities at first, but when she had realized that the Robinsons were quite competent to handle them, she had retired to the privacy of her cabin, preferring to be alone rather than mingle with a crowd.

Several insights into her own nature struck her all at once.

While she was not a solitary person, neither was she a *people* person. She didn't need a mob around her, only the company of a few close friends.

That had been a major failing in her marriage, the fact that Byron had to have lots of people around him all of the time and she didn't. They were mismatched from the start.

So why had she decided she wanted another husband?

A flash of self-knowledge reminded her that while she was often alone, she had rarely been lonely. There were always interesting things to be done— work that she enjoyed, tons of books that she hadn't yet had a chance to read, places she wanted to see.

Had she really wanted a husband? Or was it only Tor who stirred this need in her?

Yes, that was it; the final truth dawned on her. It was Tor. She had wanted *him* in the role of husband, not just anybody. She wanted him in all the places in her life, not just occasionally.

She sighed, knowing she couldn't have him and

that she didn't want to continue in their old relationship. So where did that leave her? She couldn't
rationalize her love away this time. Rejecting sadness, she looked at the mountains and tried to find
solace.

The cold air circulated around her huddled form.
She went inside, heated the oven, and put the dough
in to bake.

Setting the timer, she returned to the living room
sofa. As she watched the flames licking over the
logs, her mind was curiously empty, as if no thought
were important enough to disturb her homecoming
. . . as if she had gone beyond thought, beyond pain
even. There was a strange tranquility, as if life had
stopped, and her lashes drifted down, as soft as
snowflakes, to rest on her cheeks.

Cold lips nudged hers apart and colder hands
slipped inside her robe, warming themselves at her
breasts.

"Tor," she murmured when he raised his head.
Then, *"Tor!"* as she remembered.

"Hello, babe," he said deeply. He chuckled. "I
finally caught you as I dreamed I would—asleep and
with the door unlocked so I could sneak in and kiss
you awake."

She shrank against the sofa back. "You're not
supposed to be here," she cried, her carefully nur-
tured peace shattered by his appearance.

"Where else would I be when my woman is here?"
he asked.

"I'm not—"

"Oh yes you are, Meli O'Connor . . . soon to be Halliday, I hope." His grin went a little crooked.

"You don't know what you're saying," she told him. She hadn't realized he would go to these lengths to get his way!

Kneeling before her on the hearth rug, he solemnly took her hands. "Will you marry me, sweet witch of the north?"

Her face was stern. "You're not very funny." Scrambling past him, she rose and went to the kitchen to check the bread.

Wearing oven mitts, she removed the sweet-smelling loaf from the oven and turned the heat off. Tor followed her into the kitchen, where he sat in his place at the table and watched her as she worked on the domestic task.

To Meli, as she put on a pot of coffee, this seemed right. Homey. Companionable. Fulfilling. Right.

She tried to maintain a wall of self-righteous anger with him, but her love and his proposal undermined her intentions. She couldn't take him seriously. She didn't dare.

"I really want to marry you, Meli. Really and truly," he said softly, with a child's trust in the conviction of his words and with a man's pledge behind them.

Turning, she leaned against the sink to study his serious expression. His eyes asked her to believe him. She shook her head in negation even as her lips shaped themselves into tender curves. "You were horrified when I mentioned marriage the first time. Admit it."

"Not horrified. Maybe a little shocked. And more than a little wary," he admitted. "Don't forget, I'd seen marriage from several sides and it didn't look very appealing. I didn't want to disturb things between us. But the idea grew on me . . ."

"Oh, yeah," she scoffed, but she wasn't harsh with it.

"No kidding," he protested. "Like you, I've been sort of restless this past year. I wanted something more too. I just didn't know what it was . . . until you hit me with your plan."

Soft laughter laced her words as she answered. She wouldn't let him know what his words did to her, how her heart jumped with renewed hope, only to be crushed by her practical self. "I suppose that's why you took me right up on my idea?" she inquired with wry humor. She had to find the situation amusing, or else she would cry.

"I was angry . . . and afraid. We had had two perfect years together. It seemed we were losing that. But I was also pleased, in a way."

She was skeptical and it showed.

Meli poured coffee and placed a mug at each of their places. Then she turned the cooling bread out on a cutting board and brought it over. Finally she placed two knives, the butter, and a pot of jam on the table between her place and his.

"I forgot milk," she apologized.

Waving that aside as unimportant, he continued, "I've always made all the running between us. It was flattering to be the one pursued, although I wasn't sure marriage was the answer for us. Then you hit me with that broadside." He shook his head, remembering. His eyes darkened with pain and she stared in consternation. "That hurt, Meli, when you rejected me. Who else would I think you wanted for a husband but me?"

"Egotist," she muttered, pulling out her chair.

"Yes, but a logical one. Or so I thought. I was certainly in love with you. I assumed . . . but when you said . . . well, I wasn't sure," he finished rather abstractedly, but she understood his thought patterns. "I thought I could talk you out of your notion, and then as soon as you agreed to continue our affair I would propose."

"Why?" she asked, not sure she believed any of this but wanting to very much.

"I thought that would prove you loved me."

"Oh, Tor!" she said in faint tones of dismay.

A flush swept slowly up his face. "When that didn't work, I agreed to take you to Atlanta where I could keep an eye on you and let you have your little fling. . . ."

"But you didn't," she reminded him succinctly. "You sabotaged the whole thing!"

"Well, you didn't expect me to really let you get involved with someone else, did you?" Spreading the melted butter on a slice of bread, he glared self-righteously at her.

"Yes!" she cried, angry all over again at his tactics. "Bill Jordache—"

"Was a mistake on your part. I knew he was a fake from the word go," he concluded.

She gave an inelegant snort, bit into her jam-covered snack, and chewed vigorously. "You knew no such thing," she said after a long hard silence. "You thought he was proposing."

"And I was jealous as hell. I've signed up for karate lessons."

"What for?" she asked in horror.

"So I can kick him in the chin the next time he comes near you!" he stated with a great deal of personal satisfaction.

Meli looked at her bread. She took a sip of coffee. The silence lengthened. Finally she glanced at her determined lover.

They burst into laughter.

"That's when I knew for sure that you loved me . . . pretty sure," he said. His glance at her was hesitant after he stopped smiling. He still wasn't a hundred percent positive, she saw. But his right brow lifted as he added, "He was lucky to get off so lightly. I thought you were going to attack him."

Meli touched his hand. "I do love you."

His chest heaved up and down in a deep breath. "Thank God," he said fervently. He looked at her with longing.

"You were awful to me in my bedroom after Bill left, though." She wasn't going to let him off easily.

He grimaced. "I wanted you to admit you loved me. You were crying and I envisioned a big reconciliation scene. Instead, you told me in exact words just how low your opinion of me was. I lost my temper . . . again."

Her face was forgiving. "You stopped when I cried later."

"Yes. I felt like a low-down skunk, forcing myself on you when you were obviously hurt and vulnerable. And then you came to me." His eyes glittered over her, causing little thrills to start in her skin and work their way to the very core of her being. "That was an experience I'll never forget as long as I live." He gave her an arrogant appraisal. "I'll expect similar performances in the future, now that I know what you're capable of."

She giggled some and blushed a little. Tor wiped a spot of jam off her lower lip and licked the sweetness from his finger.

Sobering, she asked, "Why did you let me leave?"

"You're stronger here," he said gently, so that she wanted to cry all over again, but with gratitude this time. "And I thought we both needed time to think. But Atlanta was so lonely without you, I couldn't wait. I had to come after you."

"Meet on my home ground," she said, her voice very husky.

"Yes." His voice rippled with undertones that conveyed so many nuances to her that she gave up sorting them out and accepted that he was, indeed, telling the truth.

They finished eating and placed their dishes in the sink, working around each other in familiar ways. He took her hand and went back to the living room with her, gravitating with a homing instinct to the hearth rug. They sat side by side, and he put an arm behind her as she leaned her head on his shoulder.

"So what happens now?" she inquired, warm and

comfortable in his embrace. Desire trickled through her in gentle cascades.

"You haven't answered my question. Are you going to marry me peacefully or is it to be a fight all the way?" he demanded, mock-gruff.

"I'll go in peace," she said solemnly.

"Then, since we've already had a long engagement, we'll make love tonight, start the arrangements to get married tomorrow, and live happily ever after."

"Where?"

His hand tugged at the tie of her robe until he had it open. Strong fingers massaged the small nipple into a rosy bud. The trickle of desire was escalating to a torrent.

"Here, Atlanta, New York. Wherever we're needed. We each still have our businesses to run . . . except we're partners from here on." His lips touched the side of her face, kissed her temple. "You were my private treasure," he said somewhat wistfully. "I used to think I had a special secret no one else knew about—although several did!—when I came up here to my mountain woman."

She was troubled by his confession.

Seeing her face, he assured her. "But nothing is as good as having you with me all the time. That was the real lesson I learned by having you in Atlanta. It brought home to me how it could be between us if we were fully committed, but I already knew the best part—the companionship of a warm, beautiful woman."

He lifted her into his lap, cradling her. She wanted to demonstrate her love for him. Lifting shaky fingers, she stroked his cheek lovingly.

He kissed her palm. Turning dark blue eyes to her, he whispered, "For me to lose you would not be to gain the world. It would be the end of everything. Life would have no meaning."

"Yes, everything is better when we're together."

His grin became lascivious, his eyes devilish all of a sudden.

"You remind me of Case," she laughed.

"He's not a bad guy. You can be friends with him," Tor replied in a lordly manner. "Now, you were about to show me those new techniques of yours . . ."

"Was I?" she asked, faking surprise as her heart accelerated to an alarming rate.

"Oh, yes, I think so. I very definitely think so!" He slipped the robe from her shoulders. "By the way, did I tell you that I'm a mature person, I like kids, and I'm absolutely terrific in bed?"

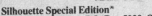

Silhouette Special Edition

$2.25 each

111 ☐ Thorne	128 ☐ Macomber	145 ☐ Wallace	162 ☐ Roberts
112 ☐ Belmont	129 ☐ Rowe	146 ☐ Thornton	163 ☐ Halston
113 ☐ Camp	130 ☐ Carr	147 ☐ Dalton	164 ☐ Ripy
114 ☐ Ripy	131 ☐ Lee	148 ☐ Gordon	165 ☐ Lee
115 ☐ Halston	132 ☐ Dailey	149 ☐ Claire	166 ☐ John
116 ☐ Roberts	133 ☐ Douglass	150 ☐ Dailey	167 ☐ Hurley
117 ☐ Converse	134 ☐ Ripy	151 ☐ Shaw	168 ☐ Thornton
118 ☐ Jackson	135 ☐ Seger	152 ☐ Adams	169 ☐ Beckman
119 ☐ Langan	136 ☐ Scott	153 ☐ Sinclair	170 ☐ Paige
120 ☐ Dixon	137 ☐ Parker	154 ☐ Malek	171 ☐ Gray
121 ☐ Shaw	138 ☐ Thornton	155 ☐ Lacey	172 ☐ Hamilton
122 ☐ Walker	139 ☐ Halston	156 ☐ Hastings	173 ☐ Belmont
123 ☐ Douglass	140 ☐ Sinclair	157 ☐ Taylor	174 ☐ Dixon
124 ☐ Mikels	141 ☐ Saxon	158 ☐ Charles	
125 ☐ Cates	142 ☐ Bergen	159 ☐ Camp	
126 ☐ Wildman	143 ☐ Bright	160 ☐ Wisdom	
127 ☐ Taylor	144 ☐ Meriwether	161 ☐ Stanford	

Silhouette Special Edition

Coming Next Month

The Law Is A Lady by Nora Roberts
When Phillip Kincaid was scouting locations for his movie, he didn't expect the long arm of the law to point him in the right irection. But Victoria Ashton, town sheriff, was just the woman he'd been waiting for.

That Other Woman by Elizabeth Neff Walker
Courtney certainly seemed to fit the stereotype of the "other woman." But when Eric Collins pursued her, she was swept off her feet like a young girl—right into a storybook romance.

Come Lie With Me by Linda Howard
Therapist Dione Kelley helped Blake Remington to walk again. So how could she believe his words of love when she knew they were only spoken out of gratitude?

Saturday's Child by Natalie Bishop
What was Jarrod doing on the set of the soap opera Brynne starred in? He *couldn't* want her back again—not when he had made it brutally clear that he didn't need an actress complicating his life.

Strictly Business by Kate Meriwether
When her father announced a contest, there was a mad scramble for Roxie's hand by the VP's of his company. Moody Todd McKendrick was the front runner, but why couldn't he be a bit more enthusiastic about winning her?

The Shadow Of Time by Lisa Jackson
Mara had believed that Shane Kennedy was dead, killed in Northern Ireland. Now he was back—and his bitterness at her apparent desertion vied with the passion still raging between them.